TRIPLE STRIKE: THREADS OF FATE

G. M. GRAY

CONTENTS

Original concept by G.M. Gray and K. Mera
Novelization by G.M. Gray

DEDICATION

To K. Mera for all those well-spent hours plotting in the high
school orchestra room

To Raven for always believing in Triple Strike

OPERATION 1: THREADS OF FATE

"We will enter the 00FG system momentarily. Please prepare for deGate."

The pleasant robot's voice was followed by several cheerful bell chimes before the faintest tremor shuddered through the ship. DeGating was a bit like turning into molasses for a fraction of a second. The world slowed and slowed until what was previously a moment extended into eternity. This brush with infinity was not so much frightening as boring — the past, present, and future collapsing into a singularity with neither anticipation nor possibility. Yet just as the sensation of boredom, extending into the past and forever going forward, became comforting, the usual flow of time reasserted itself. Reality rubber-banded back making the prior moment distant and dreamlike — as though it had never happened at all.

It was much like being gaslit by the universe.

"We have entered the 00FG system and will reach Colony 5.29 in a few hours. Please have your travel documentation ready upon arrival."

Several passengers began to stand up and stretch, shaking off the post-Gate disorientation, while Alan returned to his book. He was used to the experience and thus largely ignored it in the same way he had ignored the other ship passengers as much as manners allowed. Nothing about the muffled conversations around him caught his attention, until a child's tinny voice pricked his ears.

"Papa, Papa? Will the pyreans attack us now?"

It was not an unreasonable question. Piracy was an expected part of space travel and had been since humanity first became a multi-stellar species three hundred years prior. The advent of Gate technology made faster than light travel possible, but what had humans found on the other side of those early wormhole expeditions but intelligent, nomadic life that bore an uncanny resemblance to the Scandinavians of yore including the accents — but with pointy elf ears.

According to historical record, it had been a jarring and ridiculous experience even at the time, and all this might have felt slightly less like a cosmic joke had these space peoples not also dabbled in something similar to the ancient Scandinavian tradition of viking. As soon as pyreans figured out how to communicate "hit the deck and put your hands on your head" to humanity, they'd begun committing acts of robbery.

Welcome to the galaxy.

"Don't worry, Sweetheart," the child's father said in a reassuring tone. "They only attack merchant ships. We don't have enough valuables to make it worth their while."

Alan turned the page. His thoughts were along similar lines. Pyreans liked stealing and swashbuckling, but they weren't bloodthirsty per se. And despite their kleptomaniacal tendencies, they seemed interested in maintaining good relations with their human neighbors. It didn't bother them that humans only reciprocated because of the extreme difference in technological levels.

"Oh God..."

A murmur of confusion and panic rose from the back of the bus, rippling through the cabin in the same way the black emptiness along the port side of the vessel rippled. It should not have been possible for blackness — the absence of light — to ripple, yet somehow it managed. Given that Gating was only barely permissable within the laws of space and time, impossibility was not something to fixate on.

What concerned Alan was not physics, but the pyrean schooner punching a hole into reality alongside the bus. Human Gates required fixed locations to allow for the safe generation of wormholes between any two points. Single-point Gating had been necessary in the beginning to build out the initial colonies, but it was dangerous and prone to failure. After signing several treaties with the pyreans that allowed humans to travel on pyrean merchant vessels, single-point Gating had been made illegal by the fledging Human International Alliance, which acted as a regulatory body for interstellar human activity. In the two and a half centuries since, human technology in the area of wormholes had not advanced much further.

Pyrean Gating was a different matter. Pyrean-made Gates worked within the ship's engine, acting as both a starting point and a destination. In practical terms, this meant pyrean vessels could Gate wherever they damn well pleased. At the moment, they'd chosen to strike an inter-solar bus halfway between the human-made Gate and its destination colony. Human defenses would come, but time was on the pyreans' side.

Alan sighed but didn't put down his book. Work left him little time for "fun" reading, and he'd hoped to finish this one before arriving in port. As he considered a variety of factors, such as whether this strike would give him more or less time to finish, the chances of him or anyone else dying, and if he was expected to do something heroic, the passenger beside him started to tremble.

"No," the man mumbled. "Not here, not now."

Alan side-eyed his neighbor. The man was sweating. His hands shook, and his eyes darted with fear. This in itself was nothing. Many other passengers were moaning and crying. Piracy was little more than a lark to pyreans, but most human civilians, particularly those traveling from the inner systems around Earth to remote regions like the 5.29-00FG colony nearer the heart of the galaxy, lived in fear of the pyrean menace.

Yet the man beside him displayed a different sort of fear. He was in his mid-thirties, with short-cropped hair, several notable facial scars, and wearing a nondescript pea coat. None of these qualities confirmed he was a star sailor by trade, but they implied it. If that were the case, his fear was out of proportion.

Unless...

Alan's eyes narrowed as he regarded the heavy briefcase sitting in the man's lap. The briefcase had a handcuff — something Alan noticed but thought nothing of upon the voyage's start. Then, like now, it hadn't been attached to the man's wrist. At the time, Alan assumed the man's business had been concluded and the cuff was no longer necessary.

A pyrean outrigger flew past the porthole. Alan's eyes darted to watch it, and in that moment, he felt a hand snatch at his arm, the metal cuff securing around his wrist with a solid *chink*.

"What the —"

Alan jerked his hand back with an angry snarl, but it was too late. The cuff clicked shut, locking into place around his wrist.

Titanium alloy, he realized with a sinking feeling. Alan glared at the man beside him, but before he could unleash a string of expletives and maybe demand an explanation, the man grabbed him by the cuffed arm.

"Listen carefully," the man whispered, and only the urgency in his tone kept Alan from decking him. "Inside this briefcase is technology stolen from the pyreans. If you have any sense of self-preservation, I'd suggest you don't let those dogs find out about it."

Alan's breath caught. He opened his mouth to ask for some sort of clarification, but he realized just as quickly how futile that would be. This man was throwing him under the bus. Perhaps a literal bus, depending on what was in this briefcase. The pyreans were not bloodthirsty, but they were practical, and pirate crews took Pyrean Maritime Law seriously. Keel-hauling was still on the books when it came to traitors, mutineers, and spies.

"Okay people, we're going to make this as quick and painless as possible," a voice called through the loudspeaker in Interplanetary Standard. A Boarder clicked into the stern's hatch. The sounds of pressurization hissed through the cabin as the speaker continued in a cheery tone, "Remain in your seats and don't try anything heroic, 'kay? Would hate to ruin this lovely morning we're all having."

Alan scrambled, looking to hide the briefcase enough to pass a cursory inspection. He knew everything rode on his luck today, but there was little else to turn this situation to his advantage. With so few options, he settled for having the briefcase in his lap, his coat draped across it. With a little care, he could cover both the illicit luggage and the handcuff while not looking too suspicious. He placed his book open-face down across the coat as though this strike had interrupted his reading. Which, to be fair, it had.

The hatch door opened.

"Shall we get this party started?"

Alan didn't turn to look at the boarding crew, but the voice that spoke was young. Whoever was speaking sounded light-hearted and just a little mischievous. It wasn't what Alan expected from a boarding party leader looking for a human with classified pyrean secrets, and to a more optimistic person, it might suggest this was nothing more than a low-stakes robbery. But Alan wasn't the hopeful type.

Booted footsteps began to clang down the aisle. The cabin passengers held their collective breath, and for once, Alan was no different. He needed to act casual. Casual but just a little afraid. Yes, he was afraid, but he was too afraid. He needed a general aura of fear in the face of uncertainty. Not the fear of an actual keel-hauling.

When the footsteps stopped by his row, Alan did his best to feign surprise. There were only three members in this boarding team. Two were older and grizzled — a man and a woman, each with an excess of scars, suggesting numerous, hard-fought encounters.

In comparison, their leader seemed youthful to the point of

childish. Alan knew pyrean appearances could be deceptive when it came to age, but Alan was confident this man was young. Probably not much more than a boy.

Alan ascertained this from his big, green eyes and shockingly tousled hair — lilac at the roots and fading to white in a way human genetics couldn't hope to imitate. Alan could tell from his cocky grin. This pyrean smiled in the way a child, untouched by the cares of the world, smiled. The smile was both innocent and teasing — completely guileless but still roguish, as though this boy knew something that the humans on board did not.

Yet the smile lacked depth. It had no substance. It was as though this boy was play-pretending pirates and merchants. In short, he looked like a fool. And he was short, physically, now that Alan got a closer look.

"You." The boy used his gun to gesture at the man beside Alan. "Get up."

Boy or no, the man complied, careful not to jostle Alan as he stepped around him, but the search was brief. It was clear there was nothing either under his seat nor on his person. Presumably another team was in the cargo hold checking through luggage, but from the boy's expression, he seemed to think this man held what he was looking for.

When the man took his seat, the boy's eyes darted to Alan's coat, narrowing with a sharp cunning that defied Alan's original assessment.

"Let's see you then."

Alan paused. He considered fighting back for all of one moment, but starting a shootout in a cabin full of civilians was not the sort of undignified end Alan intended to meet.

Rather than bother letting them search him in some sort of sham, Alan moved aside his jacket, revealing both the briefcase strapped to his wrist and his own bag.

The boy flashed a toothy grin. "Nice briefcase." He leaned over, sticking his nose uncomfortably close to Alan's face. "What's inside?"

Alan jerked back, more from the other's proximity than the question, before muttering, "Official business."

The boy pretended to be put out by the curt response, but Alan could see he was enjoying himself. "And what sort of business is that?"

Alan rubbed his wrist. With a rueful grimace, he answered in complete honesty, "It's need to know, and I didn't need to know."

"Hmph." The boy smirked. He absently twirled his pistol as though he were an old-fashioned gunslinger. "Unfortunately for you, we're in a hurry and the easiest way to find out is to blow off your hand and open it later. Are you absolutely sure this isn't jogging your memory?"

Alan smiled despite the threat. Typical pyrean to be both accommodating and hyper-violent in the same breath. It was likely he was bluffing — guns were notoriously dangerous to fire inside a pressurized cabin like this — but it was just as likely he knew the risks and didn't care. Either way, losing a hand was better than a keel-hauling.

"Trust me. If I could have avoided getting involved in this, I would have."

The boy shrugged in apology. "One of those days, huh?" He pulled out the dagger sheathed on his thigh. "So how about I just take the thumb then? We're really not interested in you. All we want is the case."

Not seeing any other options, Alan put his cuffed hand on the armrest and tried to prepare himself. Yet before the boy could bring down the knife's blade, his eyes narrowed, gaze flickering to the space between Alan and the other man. Alan followed his line of sight. Alan's sword. The boy had noticed Alan's sword.

It wasn't unusual for nobility to remain armed during travel. Firearms not designed for use in space vessels were forbidden in the cabin, but ceremonial swords were in vogue, as were stun guns made to look like flint-lock pistols.

"Ulrich," the boy said in a low voice. "Take him to the Swallow. Greta, let Sif and her boys know they have ten minutes to finish scrapping this bus's engine and picking through the cargo."

He sheathed the dagger and holstered his gun, before stepping aside so Ulrich could grab Alan by the arm and pull him from his chair. As Ulrich pushed Alan, still attached to the briefcase, down the aisle toward the stern's hatch, the boy collected Alan's sword.

"We got ten," the pyrean said to no one in particular as he looked over the sword's hilt and sheath. He continued to stroll down the aisle. "Whatever our haul, we're Gating in ten."

The other passengers offered Alan sympathetic glances and general, whispered proclamations of the pyrean menace and when would someone finally do something about those wretched dogs, but Alan did his best to ignore them. The platitudes felt hollow, especially considering the palatable sense of relief that went through the cabin once it became clear Alan was the only one they were kidnapping. The other humans felt sorry for him, yes, but even more than that, they were glad it wasn't them.

Alan sighed. That boy was a fool if he thought Alan was worth a ransom. Nobility didn't mean large sums of money in this day and age, but the boy might also not be a fool, if he had some inkling what Drachewunden was, or what it meant. And whether this worked to Alan's advantage or disadvantage, Alan couldn't begin to guess.

Given the situation, Alan would have happily asked to have his hand shot off and put this ordeal behind him, but that option appeared to be off the table.

"C'mon, boyo," Ulrich said when Alan's footsteps slowed a little too much. He shoved Alan onto the Boarder. "I'm not gonna hold yer hand the whole way."

Being taken hostage for a noble's ransom was insulting, but that they hadn't bothered to restrain Alan was even more insulting. This suggested they didn't know who they were dealing with, and that at least worked in Alan's favor.

Once across the Boarder, they stepped through the hatch into a loading dock by the schooner's cargo hold. A couple workers were moving boxes, but after a few surprised glances in Alan's direction, they returned to work and ignored him.

"The kid wants him onboard?"

These gruff words were followed by a soft, irritable exhale and the smell of smoke.

Pyrean star sailors, especially the pirate variety, didn't wear many indications of rank. This had been a great source of confusion early in the pyrean-human cultural exchange, but Alan knew what to look for. While the cigarette suggested a delinquent deckhand, Alan could see the telltale hooped earrings speaking of multiple officer assignments.

He was older and grizzled with dark skin, hair, and eyes. Up his arms ran black tribal tattoos, a blend of images and calligraphic writings, suggesting Merdael heritage. That was unusual on this sort of vessel. The Merdael tribe was not known for its love of the Pyrean Navy.

His garb too was unusual. Most pyrean pirates favored loose, baggy shirts and jaunty vests reminiscent of the Age of Sail (a period of human history far more romanticized by this alien species than humans had managed themselves), or the heavy, formal pea coats used by human sailors. This man wore something quite different for either of those. His coat was dark, high-collared, and sleeveless. Though the tails were long, the front rode high, and a hint of belly peeked out, adding to the tousled, unkempt aura.

Yet he held himself with the casual confidence of someone in charge. He offered his cigarette to Ulrich, who was also an officer now that Alan had a moment to look over his earrings. Gun still trained on Alan, Ulrich accepted the smoke and took a long drag. Pyrean ships had a lower oxygen level in the air supply than human vessels, as well as better filtration systems, but the sight of open sparks still made Alan tense.

"Surprised me too," he murmured, breathing out a puff of smoke. "But as soon as Sif finishes, we jet."

"Hey, hey!" A cheerful voice called from across the Boarder.

The boarding party leader all but skipped down the gangplank between ships. He had Alan's sword held loosely in one hand as if he didn't have a care in the world.

It wasn't the best chance, but it was as good as Alan would get.

In one fluid motion, he darted past Ulrich and the boy, drawing his sword in the process. Drachewunden sang as he came free from the scabbard. Drachewunden, Alan's sabre, was designed to slash rather than stab, so it made an ideal weapon to place at the boarding party leader's throat. Alan gripped the boy's shoulder with his other hand.

"Nobody move."

Everyone in the room drew a gun except the Merdael officer, who regarded Alan with a bored, unimpressed expression.

"Put down the guns," Alan said, this time in United Pyrean rather than Interplanetary Standard. "Or I will kill him and use his body as a shield."

Time was of the essence. He needed to get back to the ship before Sif and her "boys" finished their work and started across the Boarder. This gangplank was the only way off of (and onto) the human bus.

The Merdael man cocked an eyebrow at Alan's words before sighing. "Everyone, drop 'em."

The other crew members in the cargo area dropped their guns. Alan nodded, edging back step by step across the Boarder. The boy he'd taken hostage showed no indication of resisting, much to Alan's relief.

"I'll send this one back across as soon as I'm safely on board the human vessel," Alan said to indicate there was no need to escalate hostilities. "We'll wait, though, until human reinforcements are a little closer. Hopefully this will encourage you to take your spoils and leave without creating any more fuss."

Probably Alan was honor-bound to try capturing this vessel, but that seemed ambitious and impractical. This was a much more reasonable trade. Yet if anyone here intended to accept it, they didn't acknowledge Alan's words.

Alan took another step back, eyes flickering to the Merdael officer. "Well?"

Despite Drachewunden being at his throat, the boy let out a bark of laughter.

"You're not bad," he admitted. The way the boy spoke gave Alan a sinking feeling. "But you should know pyreans hate taking orders from rats."

The boy's left arm shot up, pushing the blade off of his throat. While his right hand was in a more typical glove, the left was protected by a custom bracer. From the sound it made as Drachewunden's edge sheared along the metal, it was constructed with a durable alloy. Alan tried to pull the pyrean boy off balance, but he was more nimble than Alan expected.

With an ease that defied his small stature and youthful appearance, the boy wrist-locked the weapon from Alan's grip then sent Alan flying in a text-book shoulder throw. If Alan's head hadn't hit the deck quite so hard, he would have been impressed.

But as his brain rattled and his vision tunneled to black, he heard the boy say, "Ian, help Sif get the cargo across. Tell Valtra we're Gating in five."

The boy peered down at Alan with an amused grin.

"Maybe this isn't the best time, but..." The boy trailed off with a wink before saying, "Welcome aboard!"

The area of Alan's vision dwindled into nothing.

Operation 2: Welcome Aboard

ALAN FELT groggy as consciousness returned. Sound and touch came back before vision, so before he could tell who or why, he could tell something was shaking him.

"Hey. Hey. Are you awake yet?"

With a groan, Alan managed to open his eyes. The world came into focus, and Alan immediately regretted it. He stared up into the pyrean boy's face. The events preceding unconsciousness came back to him as he looked into those big, gleaming eyes. It hadn't been a dream then. Or perhaps Alan had died and this pirate had followed him into Alan's own personal hell to continue tormenting him. Either way, the boy's face was far too close to his own.

"Geeehh!" Alan managed to say, scooting along the floor with no attempt at dignity as he made space.

The boy flashed a toothy grin and rose from leaning over Alan.

"Hey, Ian!" he shouted. "He's awake! He seems fine too!"

Alan regarded the boy with a sour glare. Alan must have passed out for only a moment, but the world was disorienting enough without this boy adding to the chaos. If the boy sensed

Alan wanted some personal space, he was doing a great job of ignoring it.

"It's good you're awake, 'cuz first we thought you'd gotten concussed," he began to yammer at Alan in Interplanetary Standard. "But it didn't look like it, so I kept wondering how long you were gonna sleep. It wasn't more than seven, maybe eight, SP minutes, but it felt like you might be out all day, yeah? I can't say I really know how humans work, and you weren't responding when I was —"

"Sven," the Merdael officer, presumably Ian, cut in. "Shut up."

Alan almost sobbed in relief. "I'll do anything," he said, reaching a desperate hand toward Ian. "I'll tell you anything. Just make him stop talking."

Sven gasped as though Alan had hurt his feelings. Ian flashed a sympathetic grin. "Sorry, princess. Can't save you this time. I'm only here to take off that handcuff."

He held a small tool that looked a bit like a screwdriver, but when he placed it along the handcuff's seam, it let out a high pitched whine. Moments later, the cuff popped open.

"This was simple enough, but I haven't seen a lock like the one on this briefcase," Ian admitted to Sven. "If you want the goods undamaged, we'll need special tools. I'll see what we've got in the workshop."

Ian gave the briefcase an affectionate pat before strolling away, leaving Alan alone with Sven.

Sven sighed as he ran a rueful hand through his hair. "You're making my life difficult, human."

Alan grimaced, rubbing his wrist where the cuff had chafed. "Feel free to send me back to my vessel at any time."

"That...is not as easy as you make it sound," Sven admitted with an apologetic shrug.

For the first time, Alan noticed the rumble of the engines. He'd never been on a pyrean naval vessel in Gatespace before, but the engine sounds, along with the ship vibrations, were what he expected from both human-built and pyrean merchant-class vessels in Gatespace.

There was no escape then. Since pyrean vessels Gated without fixed starting and ending points, they could travel anywhere without leaving behind a signal trace — at least not any signal trace that humans had been able to discern.

There was nothing for Alan to do but either wait for a spy's death, or attempt to sabotage the ship in one last blaze of glory. Blazes of glory were not Alan's style, but neither was getting keel-hauled in Gatespace.

As Alan debated between these two subpar options, a girl's voice called from down the hallway, "Sven! Sveeeeen!"

Swift footsteps echoed across the loading dock. Right as Sven managed to turn, the girl all but tackled him in a giant hug.

"You're back! Did you have fun? Did you bring me a gift?"

She looked younger than Sven, whatever that meant in terms of pyrean years, but although she had long, curly blonde hair rather than the lilac wisps of Sven's chaotic haircut, they otherwise looked alike. The same pale complexion, bright green eyes, and heart-shaped faces. While none of these were unusual traits among certain pyrean tribes, they also shared that same broad, toothy grin that indicated a carefree, charmed life. Alan didn't doubt for a moment they were siblings.

"Hahaha," Sven laughed, giving her head a gentle pat. "Er...him, I guess?"

Alan tried to step back, but there was only so far he could go in a pyrean loading dock. The girl's eyes fixed on him with the same intensity that Sven's had earlier. It was a look that suggested a level of affection and lack of personal space Alan wasn't prepared to deal with a second time.

"Whoa! He's cute!" She slipped her arm through Alan's arm. "Can I name him?"

Alan neatly backed up to create some semblance of space between them before taking her hand. He gave it a light kiss, doing his best to keep this as formal as possible. "My name is

Alan Beringer of the House Beringer. Pleased to meet you, Miss..."

She blushed as though this were the most romantic experience she'd had. "N-Natalia. Natalia Jiordson."

Alan blinked. Jiordson. Like the admiral. It wasn't an uncommon surname within the Fimmel tribe, but that would mean —

"And this is my brother," Natalia said, cutting off Alan's train of thought when she grabbed the collar of Sven's vest and dragged him before Alan. "Sven."

Sven laughed a little self-consciously. So even he had limits and could know embarrassment. "Eheheh, pleased to meet you."

"Believe me," Alan murmured. "The pleasure is all yours."

Ian returned, strolling past a cargo crate that was being moved out of the docks and into the main hold.

"And I'm Ian, Chief Engineer," he said. "Now I hate to interrupt this obvious chemistry happening, but we have a lot of work here, and you three are in the way."

Alan cleared his throat. "Yes, about business. I need to speak to the captain to discuss my ransom."

"Eheheh," Sven laughed again. "I, er, I...don't think he's planning on ransoming you."

Alan raised an eyebrow. "If I wanted to know what you think, I'd...well...to be honest, I can't imagine caring what you think, so let's just leave it at that. Now. Get me to the captain." He narrowed his eye, giving Sven a supercilious sneer. "Deckswabber."

"Deck...swabber?" Sven regarded Alan with shock, his expression turning into that of a kicked puppy. "You...you don't have to be so mean, Alan."

"Deckswabber," Alan repeated with a vicious smile. Taking his frustration on some random crew member was neither wise nor kind, but he couldn't help feeling a little justified taking it out on Sven in particular, who'd dragged him here in the first place.

Neither Ian nor Natalia came to Sven's defense, but a well-timed voice called from the cargo hold door, "Hey, Captain!"

A woman carrying a work-tablet dodged a couple deckhands that were moving a pallet of cargo. She looked young — petite with the pale hair, skin, and eyes that many humans stereotyped as "pyrean" qualities — but her body and face were covered in a mess of scars that suggested she'd seen the full horrors of space. She gave Sven a warm, motherly look as she walked toward them.

"You ready for me to move the supplies? I've taken an initial inventory and we have space cleared for everything."

Sven's expression smoothed in an instant. "Oh, you finished already? Sorry, Sif, I know we're in the way. We were trying to figure out where to put the prisoner, but go ahead and start unpacking."

Sif's affectionate smile implied that she was quite a bit older than her youthful face suggested.

"Aye-aye, Captain." She waved at a pair of deckhands on the other side of the cargo hold door. "Let's go, boys!"

As the pair began to load up the crates for storage, Alan stared in horror as Sif pulled Sven aside to discuss the loot stolen from the bus. Natalia followed them, seemingly having lost interest in Alan. She tried to peek over Sif's shoulder to see the inventory list.

Alan wasn't superstitious per se, but he was willing to believe the cosmos had a wicked sense of humor. Alan did what he should have done upon seeing Sven for the first time, which was check the boy's earrings. For each ship a Pyrean Navy crew member sailed, they received a stud in the right ear. For the officer positions held, they received a ring in the left ear. Sven's hair was such a shaggy mess that Alan hadn't been able to discern his left ear, nor had he thought to check, having assumed Sven to be just another boarding crew member.

If Alan squinted, staring at Sven for an uncomfortably long time, he could make out the faintest shine of a ring in the boy's left ear.

Ian patted Alan on the shoulder. "I know it's kind of a shock, but Sven is an honor to his clan. You'd be wise not to underestimate him."

Alan pinched the bridge of his nose. He'd had extensive studies in pyrean naval culture, but it hadn't prepared him for this moment. He wondered whether this was the sort of thing that the textbooks left out, or if he'd managed to get kidnapped by the only dysfunctional pirate vessel in the galaxy.

When Sif stepped away to return to the unloading, Sven and Natalia exchanged a few words before Natalia skipped off to assist with the cargo. Sven turned back to Alan.

"Okay. I've got some good news, and some bad news, and finally some good news."

"Oh no."

Sven ignored Alan's distressed murmur, counting out each piece of news on a gloved finger. "First, the good news is, I am willing to believe you were not aware of the contents of the briefcase. Given what we know about your neighbor on that transport, I suspect you were in the wrong place at the wrong time. So all-in-all, I'm glad I didn't cut your thumb off?"

"Um, thank you?"

"The bad news is, I wasn't planning on taking anyone prisoner, not even that FG spy, and I'd feel bad putting you in the brig if you're just as much of a victim as we are. But, uh, since you are here, we do need to find a place to keep you safe."

And keep the ship safe from Alan, Sven didn't add. Alan crossed his arms. "So the final good news is...?"

Sven pumped his fist with excitement. "I have an idea!"

"In...your bedroom?" Alan felt the blood drain from his face as he stared at the accommodations.

Sven's earlier confidence faded. "It seemed like a good idea at the time." He put his hands on his hips. "I mean, it has a spare bed. Besides, you wouldn't want to stay in the brig or a closet or something like that. You're our guest."

Guest. Alan wondered if that was what this boy called all his prisoners.

In Sven's defense, the room did have two beds. Neither was particularly luxurious but that was to be expected on most starfaring vessels, and pyrean naval vessels in particular. Given the nature of Gate-travel, as well as the potential for skirmishes, things needed to be fixed in place, which left less possibility for the accumulation of "stuff."

Besides the beds, the room was furnished with a small table covered in half-eaten snack bags of puffed grains and dried fruit, several sitting cushions strewn around the room, a line of cabinets built into the walls, and a small desk and chair in the corner by another door that presumably led to a head. On the opposite wall from the door, a porthole gazed out into the blackness of Gatespace.

There was nothing remarkable or unusual here, except for the room's one corner that looked like some sort of nature shrine. There was a bowl of water inset into a mossy bed, connected to a jumble of sticks. Alan tried to recall any information he could on pyreans and miniature gardens, but nothing came to mind.

"I know it's not much, but I have the biggest quarters on the Swallow." When Alan said nothing, Sven shrugged. "Anyway don't do anything stupid. These are just my quarters, remember? Nothing secret or valuable here. I'll be back in a little bit."

Alan stared out the porthole. They were still in Gatespace. He wondered how far they were traveling in this one jump. Too far for Alan to get home regardless. "Home" had always been an abstract concept given that Alan spent most of his time hopping between colonies in the outer territories, yet in this moment, that word became even more intangible. This was no business trip, and he was at the mercy of this crew.

"Oh!" Sven added as he palmed open the door. "And if you see Eric, don't let him bully you."

"Eric?"

The door shut. Alan walked over to it and tried keying open the door, but the light flickered negative, the door remaining locked. Of course. It was too much to expect such a good stroke of fortune when he'd rolled nothing but snake eyes all day.

"Damn."

Alan leaned against the door with a sigh. Taking a nap seemed as good an idea as any.

Sven was on his way to the communications room, when a voice called out from behind him, "Captain Jiordson!"

Sven turned with a grin. "Hey, Gunnar! How's it going?"

Gunnar flashed a shy smile. Being nobility and the youngest officer aboard, Gunnar was one of the Merry Swallow's most earnest crew members. While Gunn made a point to dress in more casual clothes to play down his social status, he couldn't quite shake the etiquette and manners of his upbringing. This had made his initial time on the Swallow difficult, but with time, the crew had come to accept his idiosyncrasies in the same way that he'd accepted theirs.

"Sir, I came to notify you that Ragnar and I found the prisoner's records," Gunnar said in a serious tone.

"Oh neat!" Sven's smile faded as he cocked his head. "But why didn't you use the comm to let me know?"

"I, er, tried, Sir," Gunnar admitted. "You had it turned off."

"Ahaha," Sven laughed, checking the device clipped to his side. "So I do. Aha. Let's hope Valtra doesn't find out and make fun of me."

Gunnar gave Sven a gentle but chiding look. He kept his hair long and just a little disheveled, hiding part of his face, but somehow this made he look even more dapper despite his best attempts.

He admitted, "First Mate Valtra is already there, so you might be out of luck."

"Drat."

"But," Gunnar added, "I think you'll find our research very interesting."

Sven nodded. If Valtra had decided she needed to be there, something very interesting indeed must have come up in Alan Beringer's records.

As they reached the door to the comms room, Gunnar palmed it open for Sven with a polite bow.

"After you, Sir."

Valtra, who'd been leaning over Ragnar to look at the monitor, turned to Sven with a cheerful, fanged grin.

"Sven! You're finally here! Keep that communicator on next time, eh? You're a captain, aren't ye?"

Sven tried not to look too sheepish at the good-natured dressing-down. Valtra had the aura of a laid back, affable big sister, but she was a model officer who held the rest of the crew, including her captain, to exacting standards. She chided him now, because it had been a minor inconvenience, but the next time he did it, he could expect a full, private lecture on professionalism.

Ragnar knew not to get involved. He gave Sven a casual salute and a murmured "Captain" before turning back to his array of monitors and typing in a few more quick commands.

Valtra folded her arms, regarding the monitors as well. "It's as you suspected, Capt. Our honored guest is not some common spy."

Ragnar offered Sven his seat. "Take a look at this, Captain. It's...unexpected."

Sven sat down and stared at the screen before him.

"See?" Valtra said.

Sven tabbed through the information. Alan Beringer. Age twenty-seven. The images and additional information about his appearance left no doubt that this was their prisoner. When Sven reached the biographical information, he paused.

"Born on Nibel?" Sven murmured. That was a predominantly pyrean planet. Certainly not the place you'd expect human nobility to be born. When he tabbed to the next page, his eyes widened. "Decorated inspector of the Elite?"

Valtra nodded. "There's no way he's some merc working for one of the FG system's HGBs."

Sven considered this new information. They'd been tasked with investigating stolen technology connected to one of the HGBs, or Human Governing Bodies, in the FG system. Having an Elite involved made the situation more, rather than less, confusing.

"But the passenger seated beside him was our man, wasn't he? Or was my dad's information on this industrial sabotage wrong?"

Valtra shook her head. "I doubt that's the case. Admiral Jiordson doesn't make those sorts of mistakes, and the Elite have their own way of doin' things. They wouldn't have bungled it this badly either. If I had to guess, I'd say Beringer was in the wrong place at the wrong time." She gave Sven a nod of acknowledgment. "As ya suspected."

Sven whistled. "But to frame an off-duty Elite inspector for stealing pyrean tech purely by chance. What are the odds?"

"Small, but we look foolish fer takin' the bait," Valtra admitted. She ran a hand through her short, blue hair with a sigh. "So while we successfully recovered the stolen technology to avoid an international incident..."

"We may have started another by getting Beringer involved," Sven concluded.

Valtra nodded. Sven was more glad than ever that he had neither shot nor stabbed Alan. The Elite was an Earth-based task force that worked through the HIA. They specialized in investigating space piracy — pyrean or otherwise.

Because of human-pyrean treaties, the "tolls" collect through the Piracy Division of the Pyrean Navy existed in a quasi-legal space. The Inter-tribal Pyrean Confederacy turned a blind eye, since pyrean privateers avoided IPC-flagged ships, but if said privateers were caught by human or ma'jenn law enforcement, the "toll collections" would not be acknowledged as a legal act, and the vessels and their crew would be subject to International Space Laws with no support from the IPC.

While this appeared to be a harsh policy, it added to the allure and romanticism of naval piracy (part of the appeal being not to get caught), and largely the Piracy Division remained unaffected by human, ma'jenn, or pyrean law enforcement.

But the Elite were different.

Although the Elite were the smallest of the human anti-piracy agencies, their efforts were effective in a way that no other agency across the three species were. Their stated mission was to investigate and prevent heinous acts of piracy, but their founding purpose had always been to smash the monopoly on space travel and trade that the pyreans maintained through acts of banditry. To exist in this space — to stand against the Pyrean Navy's Piracy Division while operating within the bounds of the human-pyrean treaties — the Elite needed to choose their battles with care. They stepped in only on larger, more egregious cases that they then proceeded to solve. During the Elite's two hundred year history, this strategy had earned them enough credibility with both the pyreans and the ma'jenn that both privateers and full-on outlaws avoided drawing their attention.

Kidnapping an Elite inspector had turned this otherwise straightforward retrieval mission into something far more politically charged, and Sven didn't need to contact his superiors to know neither human nor pyrean governments would want to deal with this.

Valtra leaned over Sven to tap a few more commands into the keyboard. "But believe it or not, it somehow gets better. This was a bit harder to track down than the other files."

As Sven scanned the additional dossier, his eyes widened. "Huh. Then he really is who I thought he was."

Sven rose from the seat. "Valt, get this information to the Admiral. Gunnar, let Ian know he has until we deGate to get that case opened with the stolen tech identified and unharmed." Sven strode to the door, but before slipping into the hallway, he added, "In the meantime I want to get a better feel for our guest."

By the time Sven returned to his quarters, Alan was in an all-out staring contest with Eric. The human, seated on the bed, glanced toward the door when Sven opened it, but just as quickly his gaze returned to face Eric.

Everything about Alan was what Sven expected from nobility. Human or pyrean, they were somehow the same despite their cultures and evolution being separated by thousands of light years. The grace with which Alan sat, the way he carried himself, his flawless accent in United Pyrean — everything about him spoke of extensive breeding and education.

He was handsome too, which made it worse. His oval face was as sharp and elegant as a statue's and just as cold. Only his warm brown skin and dark eyes softened the ice. He kept his hair long enough to pull into a small, precise ponytail, but short enough that chestnut bangs spilled out to frame his face. It was dignified but casual. The perfect haircut for a noble who also an Elite inspector. Unlike Gunnar who put obvious effort into fitting in with the crew, Alan seemed content to hold himself apart, carrying himself with a distant, haughty poise that he maintained even when staring down the iguana in front of him.

Alan had the sort of face that frustrated Sven. It was an unwelcoming facade of politeness that made room for no one else. But given Alan's heritage and occupation, there had to be more to him than just the usual noble standoffishness. Alan was a man of contradictions. His wry fearlessness had intrigued Sven from the moment they met, but in the few short minutes since, he'd somehow proven even more of a puzzle than Sven expected.

At last Alan dropped his eyes. Human nobility or no, no one could stare down Eric.

"Whatever it is...keep it away from me."

Sven couldn't help laughing at Alan's discomfort. He found Alan's expression of vague discomfort charming.

"Oh, good!" Sven replied. "You met Eric. He's my pet iguana. He's genetically modified for space travel, but he's still an iguana. I hope you're getting along."

Alan gave Sven a look. "Are we speaking the same language?"

"Of course," Sven assured him. "Eric's harmless. Just a little pushy, I promise."

Once Sven stepped into the room, and the door closed behind him, Sven gave Alan a gracious bow. "But please forgive my rudeness. I should have treated such an honored guest with the respect you deserved from the start."

Sven pulled a pair of handcuffs off his back belt and secured Alan's hands in front of him.

To Alan's credit, he didn't bother to fight or struggle, nor did he appear surprised. If anything, as much as he looked put out at being handcuffed a second time in the same day, he seemed more resigned than angry. Probably he'd wondered why it had taken this long for Sven's crew to notice.

"I suppose we'll have to tighten security," Sven mused out loud for Alan's benefit. "We've never had an Elite inspector on board before, so there isn't really a protocol."

Alan rattled the cuffs half-heartedly. "Well, now that you know, what do you intend to do?"

"In all honesty, I'd feel bad punishing you when you were kind enough to give me your actual name," Sven said with a shrug. He took a couple steps back to lean against the wall, still regarding his guest.

Alan flashed a sardonic smile. "I'm sure you would have figured it out sooner or later without my assistance."

"Always conducting yourself with dignity and honor, eh?" Sven smirked back, inwardly delighted at how readily Alan deigned to participate in verbal sparring. He couldn't help wondering what other types of sparring he might be able to goad the human into. "But then, what else should we expect from Alan von Volsung?"

When Alan went still, Sven arched an eyebrow, realizing he'd hit a nerve. Perhaps this was more than Alan had expected Sven to uncover. Sven couldn't help pressing his advantage. "You look upset at being called by your true name, but here you are carrying one of the eight surviving black swords of Nibelheim."

Alan remained silent. Unflappable. Typical nobility. It irritated Sven more than it should. He continued, "But there was always a chance you were a thief as well as a spy. Or perhaps the sword was a replica. Who'd have guessed that sword is in fact the true Drachewunden, and you are its rightful owner. Alan von Volsung. Great-grandson of Tristan von Volsung — the greatest pirate to ever —"

When Alan did react, it was faster and more violent than Sven expected. He rose from his seat and punched the wall by Sven's face in a single motion. While Alan's hands being bound lessened the impact, Sven flinched despite himself.

"I know," Alan ground out between clenched teeth, voice close to a snarl, "damn well who my great-grandfather is. And I'm well aware you hold all the power in this situation. So kill me, torture me, or leave me to die. I don't care. Just please. Cease your incessant chatter."

With visible effort Alan got his temper under control and loosened his fist. The knuckles were scraped, and it looked like a bruise was beginning to form, but Alan's expression showed no signs of pain or of his earlier anger. Back to a cold, imperturbable mask that made Sven's heart race more than it should.

"Now," Alan continued in a smooth voice that sounded more collected than his earlier outburst would suggest. "With that in mind, do we need to discuss anything else, Captain Jiordson?"

Alan met Sven's eyes with a hard, challenging look. He had the sort of face and personality that frustrated Sven the most, but it also made Alan that much more attractive. And here Sven was conveniently keeping him in his personal quarters.

Nope. Nope. Nope.

Sven forced that train of thought off the rails. There was enough political complexity involved when a privateer accidentally kidnapped an Elite Inspector without adding Natalia's romance novel plotlines into the mix.

Sven cocked his head. He was careful to keep his face professional, but he couldn't quite hide the mockery in his tone as he asked, "Are all humans this bad-tempered and demanding?"

Alan had the decency to look a little mortified, but before he could reply, Sven pushed past him with a wave. "We can discuss your personality more after my shift ends. A guard will be stationed outside the door in the meantime, of course. Bye-bye!"

Alan remained motionless for a long time after the door shut. At last he lowered his hand, which throbbed in pain. He could hear Eric scrambling up onto his bed to stare at him.

"Ow," he said, before joining Eric on the bed with a sigh.

DEAR CHIEF INSPECTOR,

I infiltrated the pyrean pirate vessel, The Merry Swallow, four Universal days ago.

While their technology is far more advanced than we suspected, their leaders seem less able than ours. They have little respect for laws or authority, and many of the crew have a "casual" attitude toward superiors.

The ship is well-equipped with the most advanced biotechnology, but this mostly means that the wildlife is strange. And while I doubt the rest of the crew is better, the captain is brash, impulsive, silly, not very bright, foolish, naive, and incompetent.

Alan opened his eyes to stare at the ceiling of the captain's quarters. The room was dark with only a couple red lights to indicate doorways and emergency panels. No longer in Gatespace, the ship had no sense of motion at all. There was only a faint hum of electronics through the walls, and beyond the outer hull was infinite, weightless emptiness. Long space voyages were nothing new to Alan, but while he'd gotten used to this ship's higher gravity levels than human vessels used, he couldn't get used to the permanent handcuffs or captivity.

For the past four days, Alan had nothing better to do than compose letters he intended to send his superior in the back of his mind and pretend this situation was intentional on his part and not an ongoing comedy of errors. Yet every time he tried to formulate a professional-sounding report on his important issues and findings, the letter drifted off topic. He found himself venting more than analyzing. Alan needed to stay focused. He needed to keep his wits about him and not let that deceptively easy-going captain get under his skin.

Alan needed to think about how to turn this situation to his advantage. With a little luck he could not only escape but perhaps capture some amount of intel in the process. He didn't need to document every petty grievance he had staying in Sven's room.

And yet...and yet...

And he snores too.

Pulling his pillow over his ears to block out at least some of Sven's rustling from the bed across the room, Alan forced his eyes closed and tried to drift back asleep. He'd worry about writing a proper report once he was back on Earth.

OPERATION 3: A CHANGE OF SCENERY

"ANY OTHER OUTSTANDING ISSUES TO DISCUSS?" Gunnar asked the room.

He glanced up to check for hands, tablet stylus poised to finish writing out the minutes should no one respond. Ragnar was Chief of Communications and therefore should have been the one taking notes during the officer meetings, but Gunnar took his own notes even when Ragnar did, and Gunnar's were more detailed and thorough. Ragnar had been happy to offload that task.

Ragnar looked up from doodling in the margin of an old-fashioned paper notebook. Black cover. Black pen. Black ink. He wore a black tank top, black boots, black pants, and black nail polish. No one on the Swallow wondered what Ragnar's favorite color was, but they did have a betting pool about whether his black hair and eyes were natural or not. This only remained a mystery, because his roommate, Gunnar, was too much of a gentleman to reveal Ragnar's grooming secrets.

"I think Valt might have something she wants to bring up," Ragnar murmured. His duties as the communications officer complete, he propped his chin on his fishnet gloves (also black), and went back to doodling.

Valtra folded her arms and took a breath. The rest of the room took a breath with her. It wasn't an official agenda item in their meeting, but it might as well have been given she'd brought it up every day for the past week.

"What about the human?"

Sven gave Ian a pleading puppy-dog look. Ian glared back, but after a moment he acquiesced with a sigh. Regardless of his grouchy, no-nonsense facade, there was almost nothing Ian wouldn't do for Sven, and they both knew it.

"We're holding him until a prisoner exchange can be arranged with the HIA," Ian said not for the first time.

The Elite Anti-Piracy Agency answered directly to the Human International Alliance, which made the situation with Alan delicate. The HIA was not a governmental body in of itself, but it worked with every human governmental body, and several pyrean ones, as it oversaw all aspects related to humanity's interstellar travel. This included Gate maintenance, interplanetary customs and immigration, and crimes involving space travel.

Elite inspectors worked in an investigative capacity on cases related to piracy as defined by the HIA. While this meant they traveled to remote sectors of the galaxy for their cases, often working with local law enforcement, they weren't fighters, nor were they directly responsible for bringing in pirate vessels. This was the first time in their organization's history that an Elite inspector had been captured as ransom, and neither side was happy about it.

Sven wasn't part of the IPC's diplomatic channels, but from what he could glean, the only reason the Pyrean Navy even thought it could get away with this gambit was because of Alan's unwitting involvement in a case of industrial espionage. The actual spy, now captured, had been in the employment of the 00FG Human Governing Body of Colony 5.29 at the time of the theft. The 5.29 HGB insisted that it wasn't involved, hadn't known, and was now taking steps to see the man brought to justice, but that didn't make it any less of an international incident, nor did it make Alan any less of a suspect as he'd been traveling to 5.29 in an unofficial advisory capacity at the time of his capture.

While both the Elite Agency and the Pyrean Navy knew Alan was a victim of circumstance, the case would need to go to an international court to prove his innocence, and neither side wanted that. It would be an additional PR disaster for the Human International Alliance, and if Beringer was found innocent (which was likely), it would embarrass the Inter-tribal Pyrean Confederacy. Thus both sides wanted this debacle resolved and forgotten as quickly as possible, but in typical naval fashion, the Piracy Division was willing to push its luck with a little blackmail.

It was times like these that Sven never felt prouder of being a privateer.

"The IPC wants the inspector out of sight until the exchange goes through," Sven said. "The Swallow works as well as any place for that."

"That made for a fine excuse when we were still cleaning up our mess in the FG system," Valtra replied in a too reasonable tone. "But the last port we docked at for repairs was in a pyrean-controlled sector. We could have handed him over to Navy police, easy as you please, and have them keep him out of the way."

When Sven opened his mouth to protest, Valtra continued in a firmer tone, "And I know yer sick of me repeatin' meself, but I'll ask again, because I've yet to get a sensible answer. Why in the falling stars is that rat on board the Swallow and not in a naval prison cell where he belongs?"

Like most Vodneel, Valtra had extended canines. These fangs were most apparent when she smiled (most of the time), or snarled (right now). Her pale skin had darkened with her irritation, its usual translucent bluish tint flushed pink. With her pale blue hair and sharp face framed by black bangs, she resembled the dangerous ocean predators the Vodneel's ancestral territories were famous for.

All eyes, expectant, turned to Sven.

Sven fidgeted with his tablet for a few moments before placing it face down on the table. "That's not really where Alan belongs," he murmured with a shrug. "A prison cell, I mean. He's the victim here, yeah?"

Ulrich rolled his eyes. "As much as an Elite can be a victim."

"He's been very reasonable about his captivity, and I think compliance should be rewarded," Sven continued. "The HIA is dragging its heels. They have a strict 'no negotiation' policy, which hasn't really been tested until now. But I suppose they made it to avoid this exact situation, now that I think about it. So Elite or no, who knows how long it'll take to arrange an exchange? I'm the one who dragged Alan into this. I guess I'd feel, er, kinda bad if...um...I made it worse for him?"

Valtra gave Sven a long, hard look. "Feel bad? We're bloody pirates, Sven. We don't feel bad for what we take, and we certainly don't feel bad for Elite plankers." When Sven dropped his eyes, mumbling half-hearted protests, she rubbed her brow with a sigh. "Sir, I swear, this better not be you hunting for yer own personal cabin boy."

Sven's eyes widened. "Valtra!"

He'd intended to sound commanding and stern, but the word escaped his lips as little more than an offended whine.

The room's reaction played out exactly as Sven feared. Ragnar chuckled like an adolescent, while Gunnar looked aghast, face heating up to a bright red. Ulrich shook his head, Ian sighed, and Katja pushed up her glasses before rising from her seat.

"And on that note," she said. "I'm pretty sure there's something that needs tending somewhere in the medical bay." Katja palmed open the door before giving the other officers a casual salute. "So I'll leave you lads and lasses to it."

"Valt, save it for the drinks tonight," Ian murmured once the door closed behind Katja. "You know that's unfair and uncalled for." He was fidgeting with a cigarette. From his expression, he was just as ready for this meeting to adjourn as Katja, so he could make his way to a smoking area of the ship, but personal loyalty toward Sven prevented him from abandoning his captain.

"Aye, it probably is," Valtra acknowledged. "But I've seen Beringer's pictures. A pretty noble boy. Probably stuck-up and standoffish too. Exactly the type the Capt can't resist."

"What?! That's not my type at all," Sven insisted.

Gunnar's face turned an even more brilliant scarlet, and he did his best to shrink into a ball.

"Oh, not like you, Gunn," Valtra clarified. "You're not nearly stuck-up enough."

"Why are you saying that's my type? It's not, Valt, it really isn't."

Having failed to melt into his chair, Gunnar settled for planting his face onto the table. Ragnar put a comforting hand on his friend's back, but it was obvious he was holding back laughter. "You gotta stop shooting from the hip, Valt. The only one getting hit is poor Gunn here."

Ulrich burst into chuckles, which in no way helped the situation.

"Ian, tell Valtra that Alan's not my type."

Ian ignored his beloved captain's request, but before the room could descend into further chaos, he rose from his seat, snapping his tablet's cover shut with a decisive *clack*.

"All right, all right. We all know nothing's gonna be accomplished now. We're done. Everyone back to their posts. Great Mother, I need a smoke."

Valtra outranked Ian in the chain of command, but no one argued when Ian gave an order. She continued to mutter how that human would be nothing but trouble just you wait, but she complied, filing out of the room with the others. Ulrich offered Valtra his quiet agreement, while Ragnar tried to cheer up the still-mortified Gunnar.

Sven trailed after them, shoulders slumped. Under normal circumstances Sven would have happily played along with the teasing and banter, but he knew, however light Valtra made of it, her concerns were serious. She did not want Alan Beringer on board, and she was not wrong. Sven wasn't such a fool as to not realize this.

"One moment, Sven," Ian said. He sat on the edge of the table, tucking the cigarette back behind an ear. That this conversation was more pressing than a smoke did not bode well for Sven.

"Ian, whatever you're about to say, I know you're right. I know we should just hand him over. I know he's nothing but a liability. But I don't want to." Sven met Ian's eyes with a hard, serious look. "I don't want to, and I'm the captain of this vessel, and I will take full responsibility if anything happens. But even if I'm making this call for entirely selfish reasons, I'm not going against my captain's instincts or experience. So I ask that you trust me in this matter, as you've trusted me all those times before."

Ian ran a hand through dark spikes of hair before breaking into a small smile. His deep, brown eyes crinkled with affection. "Of course I trust you, kiddo. Across the endless stars and through Death's veil. I just had a question was all."

"Oh." Sven's serious expression melted into a nervous laugh, but as soon as Ian spoke, Sven's smile faded.

"Is this about Tristan von Volsung?"

Sven's shoulders slumped. "No," he said, but even as he spoke, Sven knew his response to be a half-truth.

Neither Ian nor Valtra quite understood. It wasn't about Tristan von Volsung, and it wasn't because he was attracted to Alan. Both of those things were true, but neither was the reason why. The "why" was much more complicated.

Tristan von Volsung. The Pirate King of the Fifth Octant. He'd retired shortly before Sven had been born, but he remained a living legend to this day. Sven had grown up on stories of his wit, boldness, and battlefield prowess. Sven's father and sister were legends in their own right, but Tristan was the admiral that captured Sven's imagination.

Since Admiral Jiordson was an old family friend of the Volsung's, Sven had several opportunities as a child to meet Tristan, but it had never been as equals. For years, Sven had dreamed of the day when he too could grow up to be a naval officer, speak to Tristan as a peer and equal, and see the mythical Drachewunden in action.

It was so like the Fates to give Sven almost what he wanted in exactly the way he didn't want it.

"He may be a Volsung," Ian said as though reading Sven's thoughts. "But he's still a human. If you're expecting anything more than what is in front of your eyes, you're setting yourself up for disappointment."

Sven dipped his head to stare at the floor through a curtain of bangs. "But I'm not disappointed, Ian." He couldn't help a grim smile. "He's everything I'd expect from a Volsung."

"Blessed Spirits," Ian groaned. "Please tell me Valtra isn't right."

Sven gave Ian a playful smile he didn't entirely feel. "As right as you are, Ian."

As Sven started to walk out of the conference room, Ian called after him, "That's not comforting, Captain."

No, Sven mused. *No, it's not.* Yet rather than admit this, he raised a gloved hand in a vague wave, letting the door close behind him.

***

ALAN HAD NEVER DONE time in a prison, but because of his job, he was familiar with the institutions, both human and pyrean. He knew his accommodations could be worse than what he'd been given on the Swallow.

Sven no longer kept him handcuffed, and while he wasn't allowed to leave the room, Sven let Alan do as he pleased while he was out on duty. Eric proved to be an accommodating host as well. They'd taken to eating meals together when a crew member came by with their breakfasts and dinners — Alan eating the mix of fish and vegetables that the Pyrean Navy was infamous for serving, while Eric snacked on plates of fresh greens and ripe fruits.

Alan had heard rumors of pyreans genetically altering animals from across the galaxy to make them fit for perpetual space travel, but he hadn't realized the implications of this until he'd encountered Eric. Eric was an iguana — there was no debating this fact — but he was an iguana with the ability to open and close doors (which he did when he wanted privacy in the head), and as far as Alan could tell, he had his own user account on the terminal.

Eric liked to use Alan as a perch, but the one time Alan made the mistake of trying to pet Eric, the reptile rewarded him with a hiss and a glimpse of sharp teeth in his pink mouth. Message received, Alan went back to his novel, and Eric went back to his nap draped over Alan's shoulder.

Reading was the one luxury his current accommodations afforded Alan. The desk's top panel could be opened to access a small terminal and keyboard built into it, and while it locked Alan out of most of its functionality, Sven had given him access to basic uses, including a large selection of electronic books. These books included both human and pyrean works with a sprinkling of ma'jenn across a variety of languages. The works ranged from collections of short stories to epic novels as well as books of poetry.

Alan had to admit Sven had good taste — or at least had figured out Alan's taste when he'd curated this collection. While rifling through the room, Alan had found a stack of tattered print books under Sven's bed. They were in Fimmelian, but from what Alan could glean with his knowledge of United Pyrean, they were human adventure books that took place during the Age of Sail. An old pyrean joke was that the only use for humans was their money and their art, and so far nothing about Alan's captivity on a pyrean vessel contradicted this.

Sven had included plenty of human adventure novels for Alan as well, but they were the classics. Beyond the human works, the library included contemporary and ancient pyrean works, the few books of poetry and legends that pyreans had managed to wrangle from the ma'jenn, as well as non-fiction topics such as biology, mathematics, chemistry, linguistics, engineering, and information science among others. Knowledge specific to the pyreans was notably absent, but this wasn't a surprise.

The only book that seemed there specifically to mock Alan was a copy of *Innocents Abroad* in International Human. The translation appeared to have gone from English to United Pyrean before finally reaching IH making it an atrocious treatment of Twain, but the humor of the content, its butchered wording and all, wasn't lost on Alan.

During the day, Alan maintained a strict exercise routine for when a chance at escape came, before spending at least an hour or two trying to hack into the ship's systems. He'd be the first to admit these attempts were half-hearted. His work in the Elite meant he knew his way around pyrean technology, but despite appearances to the contrary, Sven wasn't actually stupid. Alan's partner, Colin, may have had half a chance if he'd been captured instead of Alan, but Alan's investigative specialties lay elsewhere. Yet Alan wasn't planning on sitting around waiting for Colin to rescue him either. If Colin succeeded in finding him before Alan succeeded in escaping, Alan would never hear the end of it.

It was approaching evening according to the Standard Pyrean clock, which was the time frame this vessel followed. Alan had yet to to get used to it after years of working in Universal, but even with his frequent miscalculations, he wasn't expecting Sven to return this early from his shift when the door opened behind Alan.

Alan's breath caught. He was in the middle of his afternoon exercise regimen and was painfully aware that with his shirt off, his tattoo was completely exposed. Despite this, he forced himself to finish his pull-up on the piping along the ceiling before lowering himself to the ground. Alan could feel Sven's eyes boring into his back as he grabbed the towel off his bed, wiping the sweat from his face and neck before slinging it over his shoulders.

"Afternoon, Jiordson," Alan said in an even tone as he turned to face his captor.

Sven leaned against the wall by the door, regarding Alan in silence. Alan couldn't claim to know Sven in a deep, intimate way, but being a prisoner in someone's bedroom for two weeks SP time had certainly accelerated the process of becoming acquainted.

Sven was cheerful. Sven liked to talk. Sven was not stupid, but he enjoyed playing the fool. Yet the way he regarded Alan now was none of those things. His bright green eyes were focused and unreadable, as though studying Alan through a microscope, or perhaps observing Alan as a cat might consider its prey. Either way, Alan didn't like it.

Alan had managed to keep the tattoo hidden this long. It was terrible luck that Sven saw it now.

"If you'll excuse me, I'd like to shower," Alan said after a long moment of silence.

Sven's face quirked into a tight smile, not at all the carefree expression Alan associated with the Swallow's captain.

"You don't need my permission."

Alan coughed, feeling even more like a fool. "That's true."

He set out a clean set of clothes, which members of the crew had been kind enough to lend him. Neither man spoke as he made his way to the head.

The head was a glorified closet, but while it might not have been luxurious in appearance, having any sort of private bathing area on a starship was decadent. The whole room was a shower with neither toilet nor wash basin separated by door or curtain. To reduce water usage, the shower generated steam along the side of the box. After a few blasts, the room accumulated enough steam to allow the bather to scrub down and rinse off.

Alan had grown accustomed to communal bathing during his years at the Academy, but he never liked it. He'd been self-conscious about his tattoo among humans, but as was now apparent, he was even more self-conscious among pyreans.

If Sven had recognized Drachewunden in a glance, there was

no way he wouldn't recognize Volsung's Dragon tattooed on Alan's shoulder. The Black Dragon of Nibelheim was the Volsung family crest, and by tradition, star sailors of the family lineage tattooed it on their backs to honor their ancestors.

Alan ran a hand through his tangle of hair as he considered the information he'd unwittingly offered Sven. Alan was a half-breed passing as full-blooded human nobility. He'd buried his matrilineal heritage, joined the Elite, and did his best to be as human as possible. Yet he carried both the sword and tattoo of the pyreans. He continued to honor his pyrean ancestors.

This was a contradiction Alan had no interest in discussing, but Sven would no doubt insist on poking at it further.

The shower's second round of steam cut off. Showers had a strict time limit even within the captain's quarters. Alan sighed and wrapped the towel around his waist.

He'd expected Sven to start pestering him as soon as he emerged, both verbally and physically as the captain seemed to have a limited concept of personal space, but by the time Alan finished his shower, Sven was lying on his bed with Eric, poking at his tablet. He'd stashed his gun and dagger in the weapons cabinet, where he also stored his personal rapier and Drachewunden. The cabinet was built into the wall and locked with a combination of Sven's biometrics and a key code that seemed to rotate combinations from Alan's observations.

The fact that Sven ignored him only made Alan feel more awkward as he pulled on the clean clothes. If decorum hadn't required he dress with care and precision, unconcerned by Sven's presence, he'd have hurried through the process. As it was, he forced himself to take his time.

"You'll be glad to know your sacrifice was entirely in vain," Sven remarked as Alan buttoned up his shirt.

"Oh?" Alan was surprised, but not unhappy, about Sven's decision to ignore the Dragon.

"It turns out the tech the FG system managed to steal was a graduate student's prototype completely unrelated to Gating technology. That briefcase contained what amounts to a cute prototype that will likely be published in international journals within the next few years anyway."

Alan began to comb out his hair. "In their defense, you certainly seemed eager to retrieve it."

"Well, we hadn't been told what they'd stolen. And the grad student was relieved to get it back." Sven sat up, setting his tablet face down on the table. "But our primary goal was to protect your people, you know."

"Hmph." Alan pulled his hair into a short ponytail.

It was an arrogant assertion, even though it was true. The HIA and IPC had a tentative relationship made more tentative as neither organization had direct control over the policies or actions of any of the independent system governments that resided throughout their sectors. If the Swallow hadn't taken care of this industrial espionage incident, the HIA might have sent in the Elite to resolve it. As an anti-piracy organization, the Elite did not distinguish between human, pyrean, or ma'jenn infractions that threatened humanity's position among the stars.

No human organization was happy with the technological gap between humans and pyreans, but human-pyrean treaties were treated with care to prevent galactic-scale conflicts. The HIA had been founded as an interstellar transportation regulatory body rather than a political agency, but it had become the de facto organization for overseeing Human Governing Bodies centuries earlier.

"This makes my situation that much more awkward, I'm sure," Alan acknowledged.

Sven laced his fingers behind his head and grinned. "You have no idea."

Alan sighed. "I'm never going home, am I?"

He glanced out the porthole window. Although Alan could see stars, he couldn't begin to guess which sector this was, much less which system. Earth had never been much of a home to him, but the realization that he had no idea where it was or when he would touch its soil again filled Alan with an unexpected yearning — a poignant sense of loss.

After a considering pause, Sven produced a pair of handcuffs from his belt. "Let's go."

Alan turned back to face Sven, not bothering to hide his open suspicion as he eyed the handcuffs.

"Um...go home? In handcuffs? What exactly are you thinking, Jiordson?"

"Not home," Sven admitted. "But on a trip. You need to get out. It may not be Earth, but it'll be a nice change from looking out this porthole."

Alan couldn't deny that. He held out his hands so Sven could cuff him. This would be his first excursion around the Swallow since his capture, and Alan wouldn't turn down the chance for a walk and intel.

As they made their way down the ship corridors, Sven kept one hand on Alan's arm. Alan couldn't tell if it was to hold him steady or remind him that Sven would not tolerate any heroic notions. Alan's balance was fine, with or without the handcuffs, and he wasn't prone to heroism, but he accepted Sven's proximity as the price he paid to see the ship.

Now that Alan wasn't being blindsided by a string of bad luck that had led to his captivity in the first place, he took care to study and memorize the corridors and doorways they passed. He knew the rough layout of Swallow-class vessels, but before now he hadn't known his exact location on the vessel. As they left the living quarters and took a lift to the upper decks, Alan could finally get his bearings.

The walk along the upper decks led to a large set of double doors, which Alan assumed would either lead to the aquaponic gardens or the maintenance tunnels connected to them. Sven placed the palm of his left hand, exposed by the bracer, onto a biometric panel. At the same time, he punched in a passcode with his gloved right hand.

"Are you sure you should be taking me to a restricted area?" Alan asked.

He wasn't unhappy about how this was playing out, but it only seemed fair to remind Sven that Alan was human and an Elite one at that.

Sven smiled. His green eyes glowed with mischief in the dim light. "Captain, remember?"

The doors slid open revealing little more than a dark maintenance closet with a ladder at the back.

Sven looked over at Alan. "I'll go first, but don't try anything."

Alan's face remained deadpan. "What exactly are you expecting me to try?"

Sven shrugged, flashing an amused smile as though he looked forward to Alan surprising him, before climbing up the hatch. Sven moved with the nimble grace Alan expected from a star sailor captain.

Alan, on the other hand, with his cuffed wrists, never felt more like a landlubber. The bindings didn't give him enough reach to hold onto more than one ladder rung, so rather than clamor with any sort of dexterity, Alan limped up like a caterpillar, getting his feet to a higher rung then crawling his hands along the side of the ladder until they could secure around the next rung.

He could see Sven looking down at him from the open hatch at the top as he clumsily pulled himself along.

"I swear if you laugh, Jiordson…"

"I wouldn't dream of it, Alan," Sven said with open amusement in his voice, but he managed not to laugh.

When Alan finally flopped his torso onto the deck above, Sven caught him by the wrists and assisted in pulling him the rest of the way through the hatch.

There were red emergency lights on the floor, but the room was otherwise dark. Alan stared into the shadows around them as

Sven closed the ladder's hatch, cutting off the last bit of light. Without the lights below, they were left in near pitch blackness.

Once Alan's eyes adjusted to the low light of the red LEDs, he could make out a sleek control panel before them, and a line of pipes and panels branching off either side that disappeared with the curve of the ship. This meant they were in the maintenance tunnels, running along the stern of the ship.

"Um, you aren't planning on killing me, are you?" Alan said only half-jokingly as he got to his feet and brushed out his pants.

He could not even begin to imagine why Sven had brought him here, until Sven moved to the control panel and tapped a couple buttons.

Starlight flooded the room as the back wall, which Alan had assumed was made of metal, went from opaque to translucent. It was similar to the material on the ship's portholes but on a scale no human vessel could imitate.

Alan could almost see the cold drop of space beneath them, so close to the outside of the ship they stood, the ship's stern curving back under them. The sea of stars and gas glittered beyond this window with a clarity Alan had only experienced during space walks.

It was awe-inspiring — beautiful in the way that only the infinite could be beautiful. Alan's throat caught. He glanced down at his companion, and despite the darkness, he could see Sven's eyes fixed on him. Watching, waiting, expectant.

Alan coughed, self-conscious under the scrutiny. "The universe is quite large, isn't it?"

Sven chuckled, "A damn sight finer than when it's dimmed by portholes, eh?"

"That's true," Alan acknowledged. "So you brought me here to stargaze? I'm glad. For a moment, I thought you were going to put me to work on the maintenance team, or dispose of my body."

"I'm sure I can find better uses for you than either of those things," Sven said, and though he spoke the words in his usual jocular tone, there was something a little sharp and dangerous in his smile that made Alan's heart skip.

But as the moment passed, so too did the sensation of standing next to a predator. Sven's eyes softened as they returned to the stars before them.

"The stars have always called to us," Sven murmured in a soft, reverent tone. "It's been this way ever since our first days on Pyre. We have a saying. 'Humans will find their answers in books, ma'jenn in their homeland, but pyreans will sail till the stars fade away and never seek answers in the first place.'"

Alan's handcuffed wrists jingled as he considered this. "So you became a pirate for the view? The looting and destruction are side-benefits?"

Sven laughed, playing along with the sarcasm in Alan's tone. "Looting and destruction are pretty fun too, don'tcha think?"

"I wouldn't know."

"Aye, that's what the Beringer says," Sven said in a quiet voice, but even with the shadows, Alan could make out Sven's gleaming eyes and fierce expression. "But what about the Volsung?"

Alan felt his stomach turn as though he'd taken a physical blow. All the pieces fell into place. This whole outing was about his Volsung heritage. Alan shouldn't have taken it personally, but it angered him for reasons he couldn't begin to understand, much less articulate.

"Pyreans are so romantic," Alan mused in a cool, haughty voice. "But if you think looking at stars will awaken something similar in me, you're mistaken." He met Sven's eyes with a hard look. "I am a human, I am Alan Beringer of the House Beringer, and I am an Elite Inspector. I never tried to conceal any of this from you. So apologies, Captain Jiordson. If you're wanting something other than that, you're wasting your time."

Sven didn't look angry or frustrated at Alan's response. Instead he regarded Alan with something closer to pity — as if Alan's words were to be mourned rather than resented.

"I met him, you know," Sven said in a serious tone, without a hint of a smile. "Tristan, I mean. You have his eyes."

Sven might as well have slapped him.

You have his eyes. The voice of Alan's mother rang in his ears.

His first year on Earth, Alan had returned to the Beringer manor with a torn shirt, black eye, and split lip. He held back tears of frustration at being betrayed by his only friends, betrayed by his pyrean heritage, betrayed by his parents who hadn't told him that he was a half-breed and that half-breeds needed to keep their mouths shut. But most of all he'd been betrayed by his great grandfather, whom his mother had idolized, and Alan, in his naïveté, idolized as well.

"I hate him," Alan had hissed back then, shoulders shaking with sobs he couldn't quite control. "He's a filthy pirate, and I hate him."

"Oh, Alai," his mother whispered, taking off the cold compress against his temple to pull him into a tight hug. "Please don't hate him. These people don't know anything about Tristan or you. He is a wonderful man, and you have his eyes. You have beautiful, kind eyes just like his."

Alan turned back to the stars and the present. "Even if I have his eyes, I'll never see what he saw." He felt his jaw clench, and only with great effort did he manage to relax it before turning back to Sven. "So...are we done here, Captain?"

Sven shifted as if he were about to say something, but a beep from his communicator interrupted him.

Rather than placing the small receiver into his ear to exclude Alan from the conversation, he tapped the device on his belt to turn on the area mic and speaker.

"What's up?"

"It's the Candid Popinjay, Capt," a woman's voice crackled through the speaker. "We received a distress signal."

Sven's voice turned more serious than Alan imagined possible.

"Where are they?"

"They're close. We can be there in ten minutes if we Gate, but if someone managed to injure a Jay..."

She didn't have to finish. Alan knew as well as Sven that Jay-class vessels were not much larger than Swallow-class ships, but they were better armored and had a more powerful armament, since they acted as supply escorts rather than light scouts.

"We can help him run if nothing else," Sven muttered. "Tell Ian to get us into Gatespace as soon as the engines are charged. I'll be on the bridge in five. Out."

Sven cut off the communication. He glanced over at Alan. Something about his posture had changed. He looked older and more mature. He looked like an actual captain.

"I don't have time to help you back to your quarters, Alan, so just...stay here. I'll come get you as soon as this is over. I promise."

Sven didn't wait for a response. He pulled open the hatch and hopped onto the ladder before Alan could so much as protest. The hatch door sealed with a loud *clang*, and for a few moments, Alan could hear the sound of Sven scrambling down the ladder then running the length of the hallway before his footsteps faded away.

Operation 4: Helping Hands

"You're kidding me," Alan hissed to no one in particular. He paced back and forth in the maintenance room as he tried to figure out what to do.

If something had happened to a pyrean naval vessel, it was serious. In the best case, the Jay had been caught by some sort of unexpected space storm. Nebula dust created dangerous electric storms, and if they were in a solar system, there was the risk of asteroid debris. Worst case, it was an ambush. Either way, Alan didn't want to be this close to the outer hull of the ship when they deGated.

He heard the sound of engines humming to life and felt a faint vibration before they entered Gatespace. Reverse molasses. Everything happened too fast and then nothing was happening at all.

Alan had ten minutes.

With the clock ticking, Alan came to a realization. He fumbled with the hatch, having decided that anywhere on the ship, even if that meant the brig, was better than here.

While the hatch wasn't locked, the door's latch assumed the person operating it had a full range of motion, which Alan did not have. It was much heavier than Alan anticipated too. He was grateful Sven wasn't here to watch him flail on the ground, spinning like confused fish as he tried to get leverage with not just his hands but his torso and legs.

When at last the hatch opened, Alan gazed down at the level beneath him. It was over a seven meter drop by his estimate, and while Alan didn't have a fear of heights, the prospect of climbing with his hands bound and no assistance wasn't pleasant. With care, Alan made his way onto the ladder.

Safety protocols dictated he should seal the hatch behind him, but after nearly falling a couple times in his attempts to reseal it, Alan at last gave up on safety. It wasn't possible with the cuffs.

Because of his slow pace, Alan was still a couple meters from the ground when he felt the timeslip of deGating. His grip remained tight, and he didn't experience any disorientation as they cut a hole back into reality, but just as he was about to resume his descent, the whole ship shuddered.

Alan was thrown from the ladder. His training kicked in, allowing him to roll into a ball to minimize the damage, but the impact from the fall still knocked the air from his lungs.

The world went black for some amount of time — short, Alan decided as he regained consciousness to the sound of sirens wailing and emergency lights flashing — but before he could get his bearings, another shudder ran through the ship. This time it was followed by a dangerous-sounding creak that echoed through the pipes above him.

Something had hit the ship, and from the Swallow's groans, this area must be close to a hull breach. Alan got to his feet and sprinted to the double doors before him. He smashed both hands against the release panel.

The sound of cannon fire echoed through the hallway. The battle happening beyond these corridors in the vacuum of space wouldn't make sound, but the firing mechanisms on the Swallow roared with enough fury to tell Alan everything he needed to know.

Although the release mechanism seemed to be working, the

double doors that led back into the main corridor groaned apart more slowly than they'd done the first time. Some of the electronics must have been damaged in the initial firefight. They were not even halfway open when another shudder rocked the ship. This time, Alan felt the impact.

The blaring alarms went from rhythmic urgency to beeping panic, and Alan could hear the sound of whooshing air above him as the maintenance area began to lose atmosphere. He glanced up at the open hatch above, then at the doors before him, which had stopped moving.

Alan wondered what atrocities against doors he must have committed to have earned the ire of every door in the galaxy, as he squeezed through the open crack in the double doors. If they were broken and couldn't reseal, he only had so long to reach the next bulkhead, which would close off once depressurization reached its threshold.

Having managed to wiggle past the door, Alan collapsed to the ground. For too long, he sat on his hands and knees, trying to understand why he was unable to move.

Cold. He was cold. An iron band tightened around his chest, making each successive breath harder than the last. The pressure in his ears had built until he could barely hear the sirens through the pounding pain. He realized his vision was beginning to tunnel, but he forced his eyes to fix on the bulkhead before him as it started to close.

Dying. He was dying. This part of the ship was dying too, and in moments it would seal off, cauterizing the wound so that the rest of the ship could survive. Not even pyreans had the technology to nullify the effects of pure space.

Alan needed to move. He stumbled forward despite his fading strength. The gravity stabilizers were beginning to give out, which worked to his advantage as he launched himself at the bulkhead door with speeds he could never have mustered in higher grav, yet they worked against him when he smashed into the door. It had already closed too much for him to squeeze through, but without leverage from his lower body, he could only cling to the door like a shipwreck survivor clinging to a piece of driftwood. Alan was helpless, but he clawed at the door anyway.

The stars have always called to us. Sven's words echoed through his throbbing headache. Poetic and sentimental. Exactly what he'd expect from a pyrean pirate with their romanticized notion of freedom and space. But Alan didn't want to die amid Sven's pretty stars. He would not be called home by them, nor would he accept such a romantic, tragic end. He'd fight against the Fates till the bitter end.

The door had closed enough that, any further, his hands would be crushed. Instincts forced him to jerk back, but before he could force himself to put his fingers back in to keep trying, a familiar gloved hand shot through.

Between the whooshing air and the painful throbbing in Alan's ears, he couldn't hear anything, but from the way Sven's hand twisted, he could imagine the nauseating sound of bone crunching and tendons snapping.

"Sven!" he screamed, but there was hardly enough air in his lungs to make the sound.

Yet somehow Sven's fingers, broken as they were, continued to move. Sven turned his wrist, leaning his full body weight against the side of the corridor.

A moment passed and the gap grew just a little. Little by little, Sven forced it open. He was straining too hard to say anything, but Alan didn't need an invitation. He scrambled under Sven's arm — a forearm's width of space to squeeze through and nothing more — before collapsing to the ground on the other side, the door resealing behind them with an audible *clang*.

ALAN MUST HAVE BLACKED out again, because by the time he managed to open his eyes, the tightness on his chest had eased and the sound of pounding had receded from his ears.

"Alan! Alan!" The voice was distant and vague but rapidly it came into focus. "Alan, wake up!"

Sven knelt beside him, supporting Alan's back with his still functional left hand. He looked at Alan with open fear, face pale and breaths shallow. Everything about Sven's appearance was raw and worn from his earlier exertion opening the bulkhead door, but despite everything, Alan couldn't help smiling. A fool of a captain. Too emotional. Too sentimental. He'd come for Alan, just as he'd promised. A flood of gratitude and warmth rushed through Alan.

He opened his mouth to say something but fell into an uncontrollable coughing fit. Sven held him as he coughed and wheezed. Alan tried again, taking big, gulping breaths of air.

"Your hand," Alan managed to croak at last. He reached for Sven's arm to get a better look at it, perhaps help dress it, but he hadn't recovered from his nausea, and his hand flopped uselessly against Sven's chest.

"It's fine," Sven said. He managed a nervous laugh as he held it up for Alan to see. "Taadaa. See? It's a prosthetic. Lost the flesh one ages ago."

Even knowing it was a prosthetic, Alan felt vaguely ill looking at the bent fingers and twisted palm.

"What...happened?"

Sven helped Alan to his feet. Only now did Alan notice that the alarms had gone silent, though the emergency lights continued to flash nervously. Sven supported Alan around the waist as they limped down the hallway. The feeling of Sven's remaining hand against his hip was weirdly intimate, but with Alan's hands still bound, a more impersonal form of assistance wasn't possible, and Alan knew he needed the support. He could feel his body starting to work again, but the effects of oxygen deprivation would take a while to dissipate.

"An ambush," Sven replied in a tense tone. "We're in Gatespace now. As soon as we deGate we're contacting Command to dispatch a squadron. The Swallow is too small and lightly armed to attempt a rescue. We got hit pretty bad upon deGating."

Alan raised an eyebrow. It was true that by Pyrean Navy standards, the schooner-class Swallowtail was one of its lightest vessels, but even it posed a threat to full squadrons of larger human vessels.

"Ma'jenn?"

Sven smiled, but it was bitter. "No, not unless they've created better jamming technology and developed more powerful munitions since the last Navy intel report. And then decided to reveal their cards in a relatively quiet sector in a small-scale ambush. No, this is pirates."

They reached the lift door. By now, Alan felt comfortable moving on his own, and he straightened up. Sven looked a little hesitant, but he released Alan's waist after a moment.

"Forgive me for sounding like a fool," Alan said, "but I thought you were a pirate."

"I'm a privateer, Inspector Beringer," Sven replied with a mischievous grin. The captain seemed happy to tease Alan instead of dwelling on the situation. "And you of all people should know the difference."

Alan did know the difference even if he were loathe to admit it. Pirates working under the Pyrean Navy's Piracy Division called themselves privateers. It meant they were informally sanctioned by the Inter-tribal Pyrean Confederacy, and therefore followed the guidelines and regulations set by the IPC. While Alan knew other pyrean bandits acted without the IPC's supervision, the Elite worked under the assumption that such groups attacked human and ma'jenn vessels rather than risking the ire of the IPC. That they'd strike pyrean vessels, much less pyrean naval vessels, was news to him.

"Bold to attack a Navy ship, though," Alan remarked.

Sven folded his arms as the lift door closed. "Yes, this is not a frequent occurrence."

As the lift began to move, Alan was silent for a long moment.

"Thank you," he said at last. "Thank you for coming back for me."

Sven rubbed the back of his neck with a sigh. "I shouldn't have left you there. It was cocky of me to assume the situation would be under control, and my arrogance put your life in danger. I'm just glad I made it in time. And that you decided not to trust me by staying there."

"And the bridge is okay with you disappearing on this personal errand?"

"It's on Valtra's watch and she's more than capable. Once I get you back to our quarters, I'll resume command from the bridge. But no pyrean is going to leave anyone — even an Elite rat — to die in space."

Time stopped for an instant as they deGated.

"I misjudged you, Captain Jiordson," Alan murmured. "I have been rude and dismissive toward you, and I apologize for —"

The alarms went off again, followed by the ship rocking. Sven stumbled into Alan, causing them to both tumble into a pile on the floor. The lift creaked to a halt with an ominous groan.

"Bloody star fall," Sven snarled with unusual ferocity. He tapped the comm on his belt, not bothering to get off of Alan. "Bridge. Report!"

Even from here, Alan could hear the string of curses and barked orders, presumably coming from Valtra, over the comm.

A moment later, Ian's voice cut into the channel. "Engine room here. We miscalculated. The Gate took us right into the heart of a meteor swarm. Crew needs to be ready for unexpected impacts in the meantime. With the electrical damage from the fire fight, it's gonna take us a while to get the Gate engines ready for another jump."

"Valt, get that message to Command in the meantime," Sven ordered. "The crew of the Popinjay is running out of time. I'm making my way to the bridge now. Out."

Alan looked around the lift. The area lights were still on but the control panel had gone dim. A slight shudder ran through the ship as meteor debris bounced off the hull. "How exactly are we going to get there?"

"We?"

Alan arched an eyebrow. "Didn't we just talk about this? Are you really going to leave me here a second time?"

Sven ran his intact hand through his hair. After a moment of consideration, he seemed to give up arguing, and his shoulders sagged. "If the lift is dead, we need to use the shaft's ladders to descend the rest of the way."

"With your broken hand and me in cuffs while meteors are smashing into the ship?" Alan asked, but the question was mostly rhetorical. He held out his hands. "Okay, but can you at least release me? You have my word on my family name — both of them — that I won't try to escape or undermine this ship during this time of crisis."

"Alan, I'm touched…" Sven said in a soft voice, eyes widening just a little. "But, uh, I have bad news."

"Oh no…"

"Yeaaah," Sven exhaled. "I lost the key when I was running back to save you. Ahahaha." Sven's embarrassed laughter set Alan's teeth on edge.

"What I said earlier about misjudging you, about apologizing for my earlier conduct," Alan muttered. "I take it all back."

Sven gave him a pitiful look, but Alan turned away to fumble with the lift's emergency hatch.

"Coming, Jiordson?"

Alan could not express how sick of ladders he was after this evening.

As it turned out, Sven's missing hand and Alan's bound wrists gave them about the same level of mobility as they lowered themselves down the shaft's emergency ladder. Every now and then, the tunnel would shake, a groan of creaking metal reverberating to remind Alan how foolish this expedition was. He looked up at Sven who followed him down the ladder. The boy's face was serious with concentration, but he didn't seem to have any second thoughts.

"Just one more level," Sven called from above. "We're almost there."

Alan had managed to lower himself by an additional rung before the next meteor struck the ship. This one must have been bigger, because the whole ship shook. Alan managed to keep his grip out of sheer desperation, but he had just enough time to realize Sven hadn't. The captain had lost his precarious grip while stepping down, and now he was falling.

Alan looped a leg around the side rail and leaned back. There was nothing graceful in how he caught Sven. He tangled one of Sven's booted legs in the short chain of his cuffs, but with no way to recover his balance, Alan fell with him. He pulled Sven's leg close to his chest, tensed his own leg to hook around the ladder as he slipped down, and his leg caught on the rung below with a painful *crack*. At the same time, the back of Sven's head smashed into the ladder, a sickening *thunk* echoing through the shaft. Sven went limp as they both inverted. Alan managed to maintain his hold on both the ladder and Sven, but the clip securing Sven's comm snapped, and the device tumbled down the shaft.

Although Sven was safe for now, Alan had no idea how to recover them from this position. The good news was that Sven was shorter than Alan by a couple heads, relatively slender, and the ship reentered Gatespace moments later. Not having to worry about more space debris was a positive.

Alan shifted until he could catch Sven's other leg, and he pulled it close against his chest. The situation was precarious, but it felt a little less tenuous now. Sven was out cold, but Alan wasn't sure if that made this easier or harder. Either way, there was no help coming for the foreseeable future, so Alan couldn't afford to wait. He needed to act.

With great effort, Alan slid his grip along Sven's legs, pulling the smaller man toward him centimeter by centimeter. While handcuffed. As he dangled from a ladder upside down. It sounded like an impressive acrobatic routine, but Alan felt like a clown as he huffed and wiggled in an attempt to move a grown man's body weight as safely as possible. At least Alan's time under house arrest in Sven's room had afforded him all that extra exercise.

It took several painful minutes, but at last Alan secured his hands around Sven's waist. He panted from the exertion, his arms trembling, and he knew he couldn't keep this up much longer. As if sensing Alan's growing desperation, Sven stirred.

"Mmm..." Sven groaned before his eyes fluttered open. "A-Alan?"

"We're safe for now. The ship is in Gatespace." Alan started with the reassuring news. "But we do need to get off this ladder very soon, or I'm going to drop you and possibly me too."

Sven looked from Alan to the ladder and then to the shaft below. His eyes narrowed. "The hatch...it's right here. Can you lift me up at all?"

Alan tried to determine how much strength he could summon back into his arms, but he nodded. "I'll try."

Putting his all into one final crunch, Alan raised them both toward the ladder. Once in range, Sven grabbed the railing with his one working hand. His wiry arm bulged as he pulled himself off of Alan and back onto the ladder. He had to all but step on Alan to wriggle out of Alan's grip, but he was careful not to dislodge Alan in the process.

Once free, Sven clambered down along the side of the ladder, hooking his right elbow around the ladder so he could free up his left hand to open the hatch. It was a relief seeing Sven slip through the hatch and back into the hallway, but Alan still had to make his own way there.

Alan copied Sven's maneuver, hooking an elbow around the side of the ladder as best he could with the handcuffs, before extracting his hooked knee with care. As he started to slide down the few meters remaining to the safety of the hallway, Sven's hand caught him around the waist and pulled him through the door.

They collapsed on the floor next to each other with no pretense of dignity. Alan stared up at the ceiling. No sirens, no warning lights. Just the cool air of a normal hallway rather than a maintenance tunnel.

Alan side-eyed Sven. "Still want to get to the bridge?"

Sven had the decency to look embarrassed as he patted his belt in search of the now missing comm. "I don't want to explain to Valtra why it took me this long to get there, or why I don't have my comm anymore. How about we go to the medical bay, avoid my officers until this concussion passes, and maybe Katja can figure out how to get those cuffs off of you?"

KATJA WAS able to remove the handcuffs. She also gave Sven a replacement for his comm, and despite his earlier insistence on hiding from his officers as long as possible, he checked in with the bridge as soon as he was able. There was nothing Valtra needed from him. Now that they were in Gatespace, it would be smooth sailing until they reached a Navy-controlled port to repair the Swallow and file a formal report.

Thus Sven didn't protest when Katja insisted they stay in the med bay while Sven recovered from his concussion and Alan from his oxygen deprivation.

Despite the damage to the ship, Sven and Alan were the only patients who needed more than bandaging or cold compresses — tasks which Katja's assistant, Daice, was more than capable of handling. The ship had been hit in an unoccupied area, primarily for maintenance, which meant Alan had been in the wrong place at the wrong time. Again. An irony that did not escape him.

When the last patient left the bay, Katja and Daice ducked into the adjoining office to file the rest of their paperwork. Alone, this time with less mortal peril, Sven and Alan lay on their respective beds in silence. Sven studied the right stump where Katja had removed the shattered remains of his prosthetic hand. That too would need to be replaced once they docked.

The captain wore an unusually rueful expression as he remarked, "You'd think you'd stop feeling your hand after a while, wouldn't you?"

Alan propped himself up on an elbow to look over at Sven. "You take off that glove every night, but I never once noticed your hand wasn't flesh and bone. I swear I've even seen you burn it picking up a hot tea mug." Alan shook his head. "I knew that pyreans have advanced prosthetics, but this is far beyond what I expected."

Sven sat up, pulling his knees to his chest. He smiled but it held no humor. "This one is...er, was a prototype. At the time, it was the latest in naval R&D. Specifically made for pilots."

"Ah," Alan said with immediate understanding. "Small ships like the outriggers rely on nerve impulses to react quickly and precisely enough to dogfight in zero-G."

"Got it in one," Sven beamed at Alan. "But that's an Elite inspector for you."

Though the comment felt a little patronizing, Alan flushed despite himself at the unexpected praise.

Sven continued, "So ace pilots need working nerves, but they're also on the front lines where accidents happen. Prosthetics like mine hook into your biological nervous system. With that hand, I could feel pressure, temperature, and pain just as I did before my accident. It was as good as the real one. Possibly better, as it demonstrated today."

Alan's eyes widened. "But if you feel pressure..."

"Yeah," Sven said with a pained chuckle. "Yeah, that really hurt. I don't wanna do that again."

Sven slumped, and his smile faded. "But truth be told, that thing was expensive, and I never deserved it in the first place. They're usually reserved for our aces, and I'm not a pilot anymore. I'm a captain. The only reason I got that prosthetic was because of my family name. Because of my parents and sister. I feel like an idiot smashing it."

"Considering what would have happened to me had you not, I'm going to disagree," Alan replied. "Except for the parts where you dropped the key, lost your comm, and got cleaned out falling from a ladder, you were the picture of dashing."

He'd meant it to be a gentle barb, but Alan found his lips curling into a genuine smile, an unexpected feeling of warmth running through him. Any other time, he would have judged Sven, a pyrean Navy captain, for acting in such a reckless and impulsive way, but perhaps because Alan was still alive — and it felt so good to be alive — Sven never looked more charming.

Yet when Sven met his eyes, rather than smile back and crack a joke as Alan expected, the captain's long ears grew red. He turned away, busying himself with complaints about the Fates and his bad luck and how resignation sounded like a better and better idea every day.

Alan blinked when he realized what was happening. Sven was blushing. The man was normally so shameless, Alan hadn't thought it possible.

"Right!" Sven said, hopping off of the bed. "I haven't thrown up in a while, so it's about time I got back to the bridge, yeah?"

"Jiordson, what are you —" Alan trailed off, realizing this was a statement, not a question.

Before Katja or Daice could get between Sven and the med bay exit, Sven had made it into the hallway. Katja threw open the office door and took off after him, shouting that she hadn't cleared him for duty. Daice, who had also poked his head out, looked after his captain and commanding officer before turning to Alan. For a long moment, they stared at each other.

"So..." Daice said as if to make conversation in the uncomfortable silence. "You're that Elite hostage?"

Alan coughed. "Yes."

"Um, and the captain was, er, supervising you before now?"

"Yes, I suppose you could call it that."

"So...I should put those handcuffs back on till he returns?"

Alan didn't mean to growl, but his next words sounded distinctively like a snarl. "Absolutely not."

Daice seemed to realize he didn't need to press the point when Alan flopped back onto the bed and buried his face in his hands.

Like many star sailors, Alan was agnostic, choosing to tentatively believe in all possible deities on the off chance that any one religion had the right of it. Thus, he started praying to every god, spirit, universal will, and fate he could think of, hoping beyond hope that the Elite would change its "no hostage negotiation" policy just for him.

He was ready to go home.

Operation 5: Friendly Wagers

The Merry Swallow's second shift was having lunch in the mess hall. This included Natalia Jiordson, who was not part of the second shift (being that she was not part of the crew), but Valtra Segel was both a crew member and on the second shift, and Nat ate when Valt ate. Natalia had joined the Swallow as an observer for a year's tour five months earlier. Observer tours were a common practice for students entering the Pyrean Naval Academy, and Valtra had agreed to have her as a roommate when Natalia put in her request. Only the captain and the first mate had private quarters on the Swallow, and with most of the bunks taken, Valtra's quarters had been the most sensible, out-of-the-way place to put a civilian.

They'd become fast friends since, having discovered a shared love of teasing Sven.

"Look at these fish and veggies!" Natalia exclaimed as though those two ingredients weren't the same across almost every meal. "Cut to resemble noodles, do you think?" She took a bite. "But the fish are fried while the veggies are tender, so it's like mixed soft noodles with crispy noodles. Unei is a genius!"

The culture shock of ship food was infamous among pre-cadet students, particularly for those who'd grown up on Pyre like

Natalia. Fish and vegetables weren't as much of a traditional pyrean cuisine as a practical side-product of space travel. While vessels would pick up some non-perishable supplies in port, the bulk of their food came from the onboard aquaponic gardens. The plants were exposed to ideal light wavelengths, generated by the ambient energy of the ship engines, while the tank's ecosystem of fish, snails, and algae provided nutrition for the plants and extra protein for the crew's diet.

As nutritionally balanced as this was, it was a massive shift from living in the IPC capital with its endless supply of spices and imports, and a rich culture of foods that relied on grains and milks to create decadent, flavorful treats.

Natalia had decided the best way to appreciate ship food was to learn every conceivable way to prepare fish, snails, and vegetables before starting her tour. These efforts had paid off. Not only had Natalia become a more than passable cook, she understood how creative and talented Unei, the ship's cook, was — perhaps more so than the crew members themselves did. Even Valtra, who'd come from a fishing tribe, respected Natalia's opinions on such dishes.

"Unei does wonders to these swampers, it's true," Valtra agreed, "But one day ya have to visit Vodnee to try a real fish. Me and me crew used to haul up sharks and serpents that would take yer arm off if they got the better of ye." Her Vodneel accent became more and more prominent as her excitement grew before she concluded with a sage nod, "Tasty bastards too."

She smiled, sharp fangs and pitch-black eyes hinting who the top predator on that moon was.

Natalia was about to take another bite, when she saw Sven at the end of the mess hall line.

"Oh, Sven! Sven!" Natalia gestured at an open seat next to them, but her brother didn't seem to notice.

He hurried from the mess hall, tray in hand, without a glance in their direction. Valtra heaved a sigh of frustration, and Natalia shoveled some food into her mouth before she could start laughing. A full-on Valtra Tirade was coming, which Nat intended to enjoy at least as much as the meal.

"Off he goes. No time for his mates now," Valtra griped. "I should go meet that Elite cabin boy, shouldn't I? Find out what the fuss is about."

Natalia finished swallowing before propping her chin on a hand. She gazed at the door Sven had left through with a dreamy look in her eyes. "The fuss is that pretty face of his. Do you think all Elite are that good-looking, or did we just luck out kidnapping Alan?"

"Not my type, Nat," Valtra shrugged. "Wouldn't know."

"You're so distrustful, Valt," Natalia said, taking another nibble of a fried fish strip. "He saved Sven's life. Even Ian is okay with him having limited access to the ship. Greta says he's been a model prisoner."

"Yeah, yeah, everyone loves the new human mascot. Attractive. Well-mannered. Completely harmless." Valtra speared a vegetable and stared at it with the mistrust she yearned to direct at Alan in person. "He's only behaving because he believes we're still negotiating with the Elite. Any day now, he thinks he's gonna get sent home as part of an under-the-table deal that the HIA never makes public."

"So what then?" Ian cut in as he came to join them, setting his tray down and sliding onto the bench next to Valtra. "As soon as Sven tells him the truth — that the HIA has cut him loose and he's on his own — Alan's gonna stage a daring escape?"

Ian gave Natalia a friendly wave, which she returned, but Valtra continued to glower at the zucchini before giving it a thoughtful chew.

"Of course. Ship mascot or no, a planker's a planker, and Beringer is an Elite planker. Make no mistake, he's trouble. That same bloody honor code that made him save Sven is gonna compel him to try to escape. And I'll feel real bad if I have to shoot him in front of Sven."

Valtra's tone suggested the last statement was a lie, and she probably wouldn't feel so much "bad" as "mildly inconvenienced."

Ian leaned forward, lacing his fingers with a wicked grin. "Let's make a wager then."

Both Natalia and Valtra looked at Ian with sudden interest. No Navy crew member could resist a wager.

"I'll bet a month's wages he won't try to escape when Sven finally tells him help ain't coming."

"Ha," Valtra smirked. "I'll take it — and your salary."

They both looked at Natalia, seeing if she wanted in. Natalia looked between them and considered what sort of wager would make this more interesting. A thought came to her, and she smiled.

"I'm on Ian's side, but since I don't have much of a stipend, I'll throw in two week of chores as a side bet: Alan will stay because of Sven."

Ian burst into laughter at her audacity, and even Valtra raised an eyebrow at such a risky gamble. "Girl, I love you like a sister, but those romance novels must have rotted your brain. You're on, Nat. Don't expect me to spare you, though, when you're scrubbing toilets."

Natalia smiled and said nothing. The Fates favored the bold, it was true, but she had a couple tricks up her sleeve. A future pirate queen needed plans for all contingencies.

———

"Arrrr...arrrrr...or is it more an 'arrrrr?'"

Alan was doing his best to ignore Sven, despite Sven trying to catch his attention by making pirate noises.

"Alan, don't ignore me. I need your feedback. Arrrr or arrrr?"

With a great degree of trepidation, Alan looked up from the physical book Sven had loaned him. Sven was grimacing, his freshly replaced hand clenched in a fist as he tried to make the face of a grizzled sea-farer. With his youthful features, the expression just looked silly.

"How the hell should I know what pirates sound like?" Alan murmured.

"You're on an anti-piracy taskforce, aren't you?"

With a huff of exasperation Alan set the book down. "Yes, and you're a pirate that I'd love nothing more than to arrest. What's your point?"

Sven gave Alan a sorrowful look as though Alan had hurt his feelings. He picked up Eric to provide himself some cold, scaly comfort. "It's not fair, Alan. You grew up on Earth, sailing along the same currents as the greatest pirates in history, but you won't help me improve at making pirate noises and doing pirate things."

"Those pirates of yore raped and murdered and pillaged," Alan said in a flat tone. "They were bad people. They did bad things. Yes, there was a little more nuance than that, but not much more than that. And anyway, they didn't say 'arrrr.'"

Sven's smiled turned just a little wicked as he scratched Eric's bumpy neck. "Yes, well, your writers left the bad parts out of their stories, so whose fault is it that pyreans are robbing you? Sounds like we're the victims of misinformation here."

Alan pinched the bridge of his nose. "I honestly don't know whether I feel safer knowing the pyreans have fools like you leading their pirate crews, or if I'm disappointed that you success-fully rob us."

Sven gave Alan his most cheerful smile as he set Eric down on the floor to wander off. "Don't forget this fool personally took you prisoner, Alan."

Alan felt the blood drain from his face before he buried his face in his hands and fell back on the bed, writhing in a moral and spiritual — if not physical — pain.

"Aaaaaaargh," he groaned.

Sven flopped next to Alan on the bed. "Hey, not bad."

His green eyes glinted with impish amusement. With those

pointy ears, the hallmark of his pyrean heritage, he certainly looked a bit like a devil. Alan glared at him through his fingers.

"You have a lot of trust that I won't murder you in your sleep, Jiordson."

"You're too practical for that," Sven said, giving the idea a dismissive wave. "Besides, we've saved each other lives now. Our bonds of camaraderie are unbreakable."

Alan regarded Sven. They were in close proximity, but Alan had gotten used to the boy's presence — the way Sven acted as though they were best friends and not captor and captive. The way Sven assumed Alan didn't mind him being in Alan's personal space.

When Alan realized he was smiling, it occurred to him that he did not, in fact, mind. Nor had he thought of Sven as his captor since the incident with the Popinjay. He'd come to enjoy their banter. Sven's good cheer and antics amused him. Being with Sven was kind of fun.

Like Colin, Alan realized.

Sven was enough like Alan's Elite partner that Alan had slipped into a comfortable sense of familiarity despite the circumstances. How easy it was to forget that Sven was the enemy when he behaved like a hyperactive, free-spirited version of Colin. Alan sat up, using the excuse of clearing his throat to turn away from Sven. He needed to try harder not to enjoy himself.

"Speaking of," Alan said, hoping to change the subject. "You never did tell me how your comrades are. The ones from the Popinjay."

"Oh?" Alan could hear Sven shifting to sit up behind him. "I didn't realize you cared, Alan."

"I'm not a monster," Alan said in a soft voice, regarding Sven out the corner of his eye. "But if it makes you feel better, assume I'm collecting intel for my eventual return to Earth."

"Yes, that's reassuring," Sven replied with a smile, but as he continued, the smile faded. "No casualties. The ship was destroyed but all hands made it to the escape pods, praise the Spirits. The Navy is launching an investigation, but that's outside the Piracy Division's purview, so I won't hear anything more unless they task us with bringing in the perpetrators."

"I'm glad there were no casualties," Alan said after an awkward pause. "Pirate or no, no one deserves to die out there."

As he thought about his own near-death experience, he couldn't suppress a small shiver.

"Thanks, Alan," Sven said with a tight smile. "I know the captain and several of his crew personally. He went to the Academy with my dad. So...it was hard when we were forced to retreat."

Sven looked down. The incident had shaken him more than he cared to admit, so Alan decided to drop it.

"What now?" Alan asked. "Back to pillaging and looting?"

Sven perked up, happy for the change in topic. "Sounds fun, huh? We're only staying in our holding pattern around Colony 23.401 until tomorrow. Then it's back to work — stealing from you poor, defenseless humans. So if you're giving thought to joining my crew, now is a great time."

"Oh," Alan replied in a bright tone. "You know how much I'd love a chance to betray my oaths, lose my honor, and sell out my entire species. What do the pay and benefits look like?"

"We pay extremely well," Sven said with a laugh, but Alan sensed tension hidden beneath his words. Alan's neck prickled. His inspector instincts insisted Sven wasn't saying something. Sven had something to hide. Given the context, that something must be related to the ongoing negotiations with the HIA.

Sven hopped off the bed and walked to the door. "I have some paperwork to finish, but I'll be back in a few hours. Want to do some fencing after?"

Alan nodded. "Why not? Though I might take a walk before then, now that I'm allowed to stretch my legs"

"You don't need my permission," Sven said with a wave. "The ship will tell you where you're allowed and not allowed."

As the door shut behind Sven, Alan took a moment to stretch

out his arms and back. He mulled over Sven's words — what the boy had said, and also what the boy had not said. If the HIA had successfully negotiated Alan's freedom, Sven would honor that. He might prefer to act like an impulsive jester, but he was still a captain and could behave as such when the situation required.

This meant either that the IPC and HIA were still in negotiations and Sven had no news for Alan, or that negotiations had failed and Sven wasn't telling Alan. But if negotiations had failed, either the IPC would have to stow Alan in some prison until it went to trial, or they'd quietly release him so he'd no longer be their problem. The first approach was a waste of resources, and the second would hurt their ability to negotiate with the HIA going forward. Alan wasn't in diplomatic channels, but it seemed like this must be a nightmare on both sides.

And Alan had to factor Colin into this equation. Alan didn't like ranking friendships with terms like "best friend" but if he had a best friend, it was, without question, Colin. Colin adored Alan, and since their Academy days, Colin had demonstrated on multiple occasions his loyalties were to Alan before they were to any institution. Even if the Chief Inspector herself told Colin to back off, to stop looking for Alan because of the political situation, Alan doubted Colin would listen. Alan hadn't doubted for a moment that Colin was searching for him, and given the right circumstances, Alan could use this to his advantage.

Alan walked the Swallow's corridors as he considered these possibilities. He appreciated the increased freedom he'd been given since the attack on the Popinjay, but it was still an uncomfortable feeling being the lone Elite inspector human on a ship controlled by pyrean pirates.

This sentiment wasn't shared by the pyreans. They'd gone from treating him first with caution, then as a fun oddity, and now as another ship fixture. Even the security team, including Ulrich and Greta, who were the two crew members directly involved in Alan's kidnapping, gave him friendly nods when they saw him in the hallway. It was as though they'd done him a favor bringing him on board, and it hadn't been in any way against his will.

Despite having been born on a primarily pyrean planet and raised according to many of the pyrean customs, Alan found the crew of the Merry Swallow baffling. His stroll took him beyond the living quarters and into the heart of the ship. Katja and Daice passed him, their arms full of a mix of medical supplies and paperwork.

"Hey, Alan!" Daice called out as though they were old friends and not just two people forced to spend several hours alone together during the most awkward hospital visit Alan had ever endured.

Alan managed a weak smile of acknowledgement, which made Katja snicker with laughter. Alan felt his cheeks grow hot, but it was oddly comforting to know at least one person on this ship realized what a joke Alan's life had become.

Repressing a sigh, Alan continued past them. It was worth the humiliation to stretch his legs, Alan reminded himself. Also worth documenting the ship's layout and studying what he could even if he didn't have full access to the Swallow. Sven had granted him visitor permissions, which amounted to a keycard that opened doors to non-restricted areas. He could access most of the corridors, communal spaces such as the mess hall and library, but things like the bridge, engine room, communications room, and most features on the terminals were inaccessible.

Even without these rooms open to him, it was a wealth of information seeing a working Pyrean Navy vessel. Sometimes Sven would take him to non-sensitive areas that were still restricted, such as the aquaponic gardens. Alan was hesitant to return to the observation deck in the maintenance area after his near-death experience there, but the gardens provided a pleasant place to relax with almost as good of a view.

As Alan debated between walking to the library, or scouting out the engine area, he realized someone was watching him. He caught a glimpse of a figure peering around the bend, and when he recognized that person's identity, he gave a gentle cough.

"Can I help you, Miss Jiordson?"

Natalia laughed in the same way Sven did when she was embarrassed. She stepped out from behind a pipe, waving at Alan.

"Ahahaha. Fancy meeting you here, Alan."

"Miss Jiordson," Alan said with a polite bow. "I hope my walk is not inconveniencing you."

"Inconveniencing?" Natalia cocked her head in confusion before understanding came. "Oh! I'm not monitoring you, if that's what you mean." She tapped her right, un-pierced ear. "Not a crew member. I'm like you."

Alan arched an eyebrow. "A prisoner?"

She flashed a wicked grin. "A hanger-on."

"I'm happy to leave whenever the crew is willing to let me go," Alan said with a haughty shrug. He started to walk away, but Natalia fell into step with him.

"I kid, I kid!" she said to assuage his feelings. "How about this? We're both here on business but in different ways?"

She grinned up at him, and Alan gave her a look, as though to convey he was hoping to have some time alone. Natalia continued to smile, doing a remarkable job of missing his cue. Like brother like sister, Alan supposed.

After a moment of consideration, Alan gave up and provided her the opening for conversation she was so clearly fishing for. "So what's your business on this ship then?"

"You don't know about the Observer System?"

Alan nodded. "I do. Students can opt to stay aboard a working vessel for a pyrean year before entering the Naval Academy."

"Right. It's a tradition that goes back to pre-Academy times. Back when you joined a ship as an apprentice and learned every-thing on the job."

"I know about this system," Alan said, "but I didn't realize they allowed cadets to join active crews working in the Piracy Division."

Natalia shrugged. "It's true. Most cadets get put on supply barges and serve terms out in the backwaters. My father, Admiral Jiordson, has a bit of a protective streak, so he wanted me to be onboard Sven's vessel. To watch over me, I guess."

Alan raised an eyebrow. "He's protective so he put you on an active pirate vessel?"

Natalia laced her fingers behind her back. "We're a pirate family, Alan. I'm going to be a pirate. If I die out in space, that's just the thread of my life being cut from the skein. What's the point running from the Fates? Papa can't stop that from happening if it's destined to happen, but he can make sure Sven is on the hook for keeping me safe in the meantime."

She gave Alan a bright, cheerful smile as though this logic were both obvious and sensible and nothing about this line of thinking concerned her in the least.

Pirates really are all insane, Alan thought to himself.

Looking up at the ceiling, Natalia continued, "I wouldn't mind skipping Academy to be honest. I just want to be sailing, even if it means more years scrubbing toilets and cleaning out the aquaponic vents before I get trusted with a ship."

"I'm guessing Admiral Jiordson doesn't want that, though," Alan murmured, having had his own share of experience with fathers and their expectations.

"No," she laughed. "No he doesn't."

All at once, she leaned into him, twining her arm around his. "What do you say, Alan? When I become a captain, want to sail with me? We can get married if you want. I won't mind."

Unsure if she was serious or teasing, Alan gently shook his arm in an attempt to dislodge her, but she didn't loosen her grip. He tried again with words. "Considering I'm already engaged, that might be awkward, Miss Jiordson."

Whenever Alan used Elaine as an excuse to stop people from hitting on him, Alan felt a small pang of guilt that he mostly ignored. Their marriage had been arranged as a political and economic convenience, but while there were no romantic feelings between them, he and Elaine had been friends since childhood. Alan held her in the highest regard. Yet this meant he knew El well enough to believe she wouldn't be too annoyed at him for taking her name in vain.

"Engaged?" Natalia's eyes widened. Her grip tightened. "Already? But it's only been three weeks since you met. How can Sven move this fast?"

"What?!" Alan yelped. "No. No, no, no. It's not like that."

Alan didn't appreciate how his face heated, as though it had forgotten it belonged to a twenty-seven year old, and not some pre-teen. He intended to recover his composure and put the subject behind him, but when Natalia leaned forward to interrogate him further, he couldn't help backing up to make space. His back touched the door panel behind him.

The lock beeped, and the door slid open. Both Natalia and Alan stopped to stare at the open hatch.

"Will you look at that," Natalia mused. "You have as high of clearance as I do. Maybe higher?"

Alan's eyes flicked to the sign by the door. It was in United Pyrean, which Alan was fluent at both speaking and reading. This was an engine storeroom. Definitely not the sort of place a prisoner, or even a guest on the ship, should access.

Natalia looked him over in silence, and when their eyes met, she mused out loud, "Are you absolutely sure you're not engaged to Sven?"

Suddenly unsure himself, Alan stammered a hasty excuse and hurried away, leaving Natalia behind as he went deeper into the engine sector of the ship. He could feel the girl's eyes on his back as he walked at a pace just shy of a jog, but she said nothing and made no attempt to catch up with him.

Somehow this made the situation more disconcerting.

Operation 6: Sightseeing

The hum of the engines grew louder as Alan ventured deeper into the ship. He'd hoped to clear his head on this walk, but instead of helping him work through the information, it had only raised more questions. His heart continued to race.

That door had been locked earlier this week, Alan was certain of it. He'd tried opening as many of the ship doors as he could after receiving the clearance to leave Sven's room, and while he might have assumed he'd simply missed this corridor, the engine rooms were one of the places that had most interested Alan. When he'd begun investigating the ship, it had been the first section he'd poked around. There was simply no way.

Something had changed. The keycard in his pocket was the same, but the permissions it gave him had been updated. This was either a stroke of incredible luck, someone on the inside was assisting him, or it was a trap.

Alan had long given up on luck, and the idea that anyone aboard the Swallow was an Elite mole was near impossible. The Elite knew how to work pyrean channels associated with the black markets and criminal rings, but even the Vanguard had never managed to crack the Navy itself. There was too much risk and too little reward any human organizations could offer people working in one of the most prestigious, well-paid positions in star sailing.

That meant it was a trap.

But was it a trap for Alan, or was Alan the bait? As Alan considered the situation, he reached over to palm open another door. The lock light turned green and the door opened. He couldn't help casting a guilty look in the direction of the nearest hallway camera before forcing the feeling down. He'd done nothing wrong. He hadn't violated any of the rules laid out before him. Even pyrean pirates weren't so capricious as to punish someone for doing a thing they'd allowed...he assumed.

It occurred to Alan that trying to approach this logically wouldn't work. He needed to think like a pirate. He tried to imagine what Sven and the other members of the crew thought about him — what they wanted from him.

There were many possibilities, but through that lens, this was likely a test. Perhaps to see if Alan's loyalties to his human heritage could be swayed by his pyrean lineage. Or perhaps Sven was just messing with him for pure entertainment value.

Regardless, Alan couldn't afford to miss this opportunity. He approached the door of the main engine room. Like the other doors, it slid open as requested, and he took a step inside. Before him stood the heart of pyrean space supremacy. Gate engines — a technology only a handful of humans had managed to study even on merchant-class pyrean vessels. Far fewer humans had seen them on this sort of naval ship.

As Alan took a couple more steps into the room, he surveyed the multitude of control panels and stations, both lining the walls and forming rows of workstations across the room's open floor-ing. The ceiling was much higher than the corridors beyond — probably three or four decks worth of height, Alan estimated. Each level had a series of catwalks allowing access to equipment along the walls, while in the center of the room stood a large pillar. It was some sort of metal structure that touched both the floor and the vaulted ceiling, likely feeding into the engines themselves.

As Alan tried to get a better look, a voice called out, "Hey! You're back already? Can you lend me a hand now? I am so far behind on this, Sif is gonna kill me."

Alan said nothing, unwilling to leave the room, but hesitant to reveal he was not whoever this engineer thought he was.

The voice called out again, this time in a more plaintive tone, "Please?"

It was so polite and pitiful, Alan couldn't help giving into the request. Alan started to walk across the room. The engineer who'd called to him was hidden behind one of the many workstations, whose layout made the floor feel like a maze. As Alan peered around the terminals, he admired the alien technology before him. The central pillar was mostly metal and carbon fiber. The panels had the smooth curves, which pyreans favored inside their vessels, unlike the outer hulls, which tended to resemble old-fash- ioned European sailing ships.

Engineering courses were a standard part of Elite education, but Alan hadn't specialized in that track enough to know how this pillar's design differed from those in civilian vessels. As he passed the pillar, he noticed clear glass portholes along the sides revealing some sort of ferrofluid spinning within the chamber.

Alan did his best to memorize the details should a human engineer need a report, but if he were honest, he didn't under- stand enough to describe much beyond what the HIA's top engi- neers already knew.

Passing a row of workstations toward the back of the room, he finally caught sight of the room's other occupant. The pyrean engineer, a young man, was sprawled out on the floor, surrounded by scattered parts and containers as he tapped at a tablet. Alan recognized him as one of the two who'd assisted Sif when Alan was first captured.

"Don't laugh at me, Lance," the man said without turning to

face Alan. "But I hooked up the crystals directly to the capacitors. We have to break all of these down and redo them."

"You'll have to walk me through the process," Alan murmured. "But if you don't mind a human helping, I have nothing but time on my hands."

The pyrean looked up with a start. "Spirits! I swore you were Lance." He sat up, pulling his knees to his chest. "Er, that's my brother. You're Alan, right? Um, I don't suppose you have clearance to be here?"

Alan sat down next to him. "For what it's worth, I don't not have clearance?"

The other man stared at Alan for a long moment before chuckling. "I suppose you did manage to get in here, huh? If the captain says it's okay, I certainly don't mind."

Although the man looked young, he didn't look as young as Sven appeared. Yet every indication of rank and experience suggested Sven must be older. It was a reminder of how difficult it was for humans to gauge pyrean age. Pyreans didn't follow the same aging process as humans despite similarities in appearance and the ability to interbreed.

The man began to sort through the crates beside him. His blonde hair was slicked back, and he had pale gray eyes. Both were common features among a handful of the pyrean tribes, but while he was nondescript by pyrean standards, he had a soft smile and gentle expression that made him quite handsome.

He opened one of the crates full of boards, before giving Alan an apologetic look. "I need to remove then reattach the crystalline converters on all of these."

Alan nodded. "I think I might remember enough from my engineering courses to help with that."

Alan walked through the steps just to confirm the process, and when the man nodded, Alan began disassembling and reassembling the boards on his own.

"I'm Dirk, by the way," the other man said after a moment of them working in silence. "I think we kinda saw each other a few weeks ago."

"Yes." Alan said, not bothering to add that at the time, Dirk had been stripping down valuables from the human vessel while Alan was being kidnapped. "Has it really only been three weeks?"

Alan replaced the crystal with care as he considered his time on the ship. Most of the time he'd spent alone in Sven's room, but looking back, it felt strangely action-packed. Perhaps the combination of a near-death experience and his rotating cast of captors made the flow of time seem chaotic.

"Feels like you've been here longer, maybe?" Dirk murmured. "Practically part of the crew, eh?"

"I'm not sure about that," Alan replied with dry smile. "But I've been here long enough that I'm trusted not to blow up the ship it seems."

Dirk shrugged. "Not sure what you'd gain by blowing up the ship while you're on it." He smiled a little as he pulled out another board. "They always tell us Elite are crazy, but I think it's like a 'dedicated' sort of crazy, not a 'blowing up ships' crazy. Us privateers are supposed to be the reckless ones."

"Yes," Alan nodded. "I will admit the level of recklessness around here is a little hard to get used to."

With a laugh, Dirk returned his attention to the last of his boards, and after a few more minutes of companionable silence, they finished rebuilding them. Dirk looked through the stack of panels to check over their work.

"Will you look at that. All done!"

After giving the boards a nod of approval, Dirk smiled at Alan and pulled on the goggles hanging around his neck. "Now I have to finish installing them before Sif comes to check on me." He pulled off the workstation panel and lay on his back to reach inside it. "Mind handing me that drill? The bit is already attached."

Alan dug through the tool kit and pulled out the loaded drill. He placed it in Dirk's outstretched hand, but after a moment of consideration, he pocketed a couple of the other tools. In between the whir of the drill, Dirk continued to chat with Alan.

"But you know, I'm not sure how you messing with these redundant navigation sensors would blow up the ship anyway. It might not be obvious, what with me messing up a whole set of boards, but I'm the most junior engineer on the Swallow. I'm even more junior than my identical twin brother who, for the record, was born after me. They don't trust me with anything system critical. Not yet, maybe not ever."

"We all have to start somewhere," Alan replied in a supportive tone.

After one last round of drilling, Dirk slid out from under the workstation. "Oh, I try to be positive about it, don't worry." He pushed up his goggles and sat up beside Alan. "Being below Lance is the only part that really gets to me. He spends all his time chasing after Agnus and bragging to any pretty girl that spares him a glance, but somehow he's still the more competent one between the two of us. It's a bitter dreg to swallow."

Alan couldn't help a laugh, but when Dirk looked a little offended, Alan clarified, "No, no, I'm not laughing at you. You just remind me of my younger brother."

Dirk pulled the nearby tablet into his lap to start up the system diagnostics. "I hope that's a good thing."

"Very much so," Alan assured him. "Lyndas is my closest sibling."

Alan thought about his handsome, hard-working brother and couldn't help a fond smile. "He used to lament that nothing came naturally to him, but he's almost certainly going to be the one to continue our family's merchant businesses."

His parents had adopted Lyndas shortly after they'd returned to Earth, so he was only a few months younger than Alan. Each in their own way had struggled to adjust to the life of gentry on Earth.

Dirk looked up from his tablet. "What about your other sibs?"

"My two sisters, Lydia and Alicia, are about five years older." Alan didn't worry about hiding family details from Dirk. Sven would have run an extensive investigation into his background by now, whether or not he chose to share the details with the rest of the crew. "They both play piano and have black belts in karate, but Lydia is a concert pianist, and Alicia runs a dojo. And then there's Chance." Alan tried not to, but he couldn't help a grimace. "He's the eldest and the heir."

Chance was a playboy and proud of it. He was also a spendthrift and layabout, but most frustrating of all, he was competent and capable at anything he put his mind to. Which mostly was drinking and flirting, yes, but he'd succeed at the social navigation and deal-making with Earth nobility that made Alan flounder.

Dirk opened his mouth to respond, but before he could, a voice cut in, "Hey, Dirk! Stop slacking off, will ya?"

A young man jogged toward them. He had long hair and a multitude of braids, but his facial features matched Dirk's.

"Agnus needs us to check a few ventilators that aren't functioning properly. When are you gonna be done with that navigation system?" He blinked as if noticing Alan for the first time. "And what's that human doing here? That's gotta be against regulations."

"Er...I thought...I just..." Dirk stuttered.

"It's all right, Dirk," a familiar voice called out from the other side of the engineering bay. Soft footsteps made their way across the floor's metal paneling. "I'll finish those tests while you help out your brother."

Ian emerged from the maze of terminals, placing a hand on Lance's shoulder as he regarded Dirk. "And I'll entertain our guest from here onward, Dirk."

"Sir!" Dirk said with a hasty salute. He scrambled to collect his gear, getting the area back into some semblance of order as Lance looked on with an impatient expression.

Ian gave Lance's shoulder a gentle shake. "And don't be so hard on your brother, Lance. Agnus won't mind a little delay."

"Sir!" Lance answered with his own wide-eyed salute.

Ian looked over the tablet data as the two brothers ran, just shy of sprinting, out the door. Whether it was out of fear of Ian, or in an attempt to impress the Chief of Engineering, Alan couldn't tell.

With a chuckle, Ian finished scrolling through the diagnostic data. "They're cute, aren't they? And it looks like you did a fine job assisting young Dirk."

He snapped the tablet closed before walking over to Alan to shut the side paneling of the workstation. "Did you enjoy your tour of the engineering room? Perhaps you want to apply for a permanent position?"

"You're the second person to offer me a job today," Alan noted with an ironic smile. "Is that why you gave me access to these restricted areas?"

"The captain wants you to feel at home, so maybe. Who knows?" he said with a shrug as if Alan having access to these areas was none of his business nor his concern. "Despite what you humans may think, we're not afraid of you stealing our secrets. You are allowed on pyrean merchant ships, aren't you?"

"Yes, but humans can rarely join as engineers."

"Probably because they're not qualified," Ian countered. He must have noticed Alan's frown, because he added, "Oh, don't give me that look. Your current technology accomplishes the same thing as ours, but it's implemented in a very different way. You can't just reverse engineer it and stick it on a ship. Even if you could, you don't have access to half of the materials needed to create the alloys we use."

"What? So if we ask nicely, you'll take us to those parts of the galaxy?"

"Doubt it," Ian said with a smile. "You humans are a nuisance, you know. You have so many strong opinions about how everything should be, and all that chaos disrupts the nice thing we had going with the ma'jenn."

Alan arched a disbelieving eyebrow. "Isn't chaos what you

'privateers' pride yourselves on? Also I'm not sure the ma'jenn would agree about your prior relationship being 'nice.'"

"Oh, they might disagree, but I think they enjoy it in their own way." Ian laughed. "If you ask me, we're doing them a favor. I can't imagine living that long and not wanting at least some day-to-day surprises."

The ma'jenn and pyreans had been cohabitating the galaxy long before humans left their solar system. This meant that, while the Piracy Division had no qualms about striking ma'jenn caravans who were in the wrong place at the wrong time, the two species maintained good relations through extensive trade and immigration treaties. Conflicts still happened, but it was localized, and each race understood the other's quirks, having adapted to accommodate the other several thousand years ago.

Another shock during the early days of human-pyrean contact was that the concept of wars, like those that had defined a large part of humanity's history, was unknown to both pyrean and ma'jenn. Small skirmishes and banditry were frequent exchanges, but the idea of ongoing conflicts fueled by ideology, resources, or retribution were alien in both species. As far as human historians could glean, there had been no galaxy-scale conflict between the two races in the history of their peoples, and any stellar conflicts were short-lived and resolved with either treaties or avoidance. When territories existed on a solar, if not galactic, scale, avoidance was actually quiet easy and practical.

The technology gap between pyrean and ma'jenn was also smaller than it was between the two dominant species and humans. While there was no denying pyreans held supremacy in the domain of star travel, the ma'jenn had comparable weaponry and more advanced technologies related to planetside agriculture, architecture, and terraforming. In comparison to these powerful civilizations, humanity was hardly a blip on the galactic radar — so much so that, while the pyreans deigned to enter into somewhat condescending treaties with the HIA, the ma'jenn refused to engage with humans in any official capacity.

"I know you privateers enjoy surprises," Alan acknowledged. "It's something I'm learning to expect."

"See? Just like the ma'jenn. Even an old dog can learn a new trick," Ian said with a smile before returning to his work. "Let me know if you have any questions. I'm sure you're dying to poke around here."

"If I had a little more background in engineering, I'm sure I would be. As it is, your secrets are probably safe." Alan gave a small bow and turned toward the exit, but after a couple steps, he hesitated. "Actually I do have one question, but it's not about your engines."

Ian paused. "Oh?"

"I know Navy crew members receive a stud for every vessel they serve on, and officers receive an additional ring." Alan peered at Ian to double check. "But you have three studs, two rings, and a clip. Sif had a clip as well. What does that mean? We weren't taught about that at the Academy."

"This thing?" Ian touched the clip wrapped around the top of his left ear. "I'm not surprised you weren't taught. It's of no strategic value, and there aren't that many out there. You get one when your ship is lost. It's for survivors."

Alan's eyes widened, realizing what a landmine he'd stepped into, but Ian's slight smile didn't waver. "Sif and I are the only Swallow members who have one. What happened to the Popinjay was unusual. The Pyrean Navy rarely loses vessels, but when a ship does go down like that, the rate of survival tends to be low."

Ian shrugged, his smile fading into a somber expression before he turned away from Alan. "Sif was lucky. I..."

Ian pulled out a cigarette. Smoking on ships wasn't common, and it was limited to specific, well-ventilated parts of a vessel. Yet Ian had no qualms lighting it up and taking a drag before he finished, "I was too busy to die."

Rather than elaborate, Ian went silent and returned to his work. His face was more subdued than before, and Alan felt guilty for bringing it up.

"I'm sorry for your loss," he murmured.

Ian didn't reply, giving only a soft grunt in response. After a long moment, curiosity got the better of politeness, and Alan asked, "The ship you were on...is it one I'd recognize?"

"Maybe," Ian admitted. "It happened a long time ago by your years." He paused as he did the mental calculations. "About thirty Standard Earth years, I reckon. He was the Crimson Raptor. The finest ship to court the Sea of Stars — after the Swallow, of course."

Alan mulled over the name. It was familiar but he couldn't recall where he'd heard it. It might have been in an Academy history course, but that was long enough ago, it was in no way a current event by human standards.

"Look it up," Ian suggested, his tone just innocuous enough to make Alan wonder if he had a plan. "It'll give you something to do. May be more informative than you realize."

"Thank you. I will."

Alan bowed before making his way to the exit. Ian didn't say anything until Alan reached to palm open the door.

"Oh, and Inspector," Ian called out. Alan turned. "If you have clearance, you really are free to wander. I can't say I know exactly what the captain is thinking, but don't be too insulted just because he doesn't perceive you as a threat."

"I know," Alan said, though he felt his jaw harden at the unspoken implication. So it wasn't so much a trap as it was Sven playing games with him. It seemed Alan was little more than an amusing toy to the crew of the Swallow.

"He thinks me harmless, and perhaps he's right," Alan said. He knew he shouldn't rise to Ian's bait, but he couldn't help it. "Perhaps there is nothing I can hope to accomplish even with a higher level of clearance."

The door opened, but Alan did not step through. He felt a sudden, sharp cut of shame and unexpected fury at how humans could be so beneath pyrean notice. Humans had spent the last three hundred years developing a sense of inadequacy and helplessness, but in this moment, it was more apparent, piercing Alan more deeply than he was used to.

He drew himself up with as much pride as he could muster, honing his cold arrogance into a blade with which to face Ian. "But I chose to become an Elite, because I believe in the Elite's mission — to free the galaxy of piracy. To break the monopoly pyreans hold over space travel and trade through their underhanded means. That is our duty. My duty. And I will do whatever I can to fulfill it."

Ian was hidden behind too many work stations for Alan to see him, but after a moment Alan heard a chuckle. "I'd expect no less, Sir Beringer."

Once Alan left the engine room, and the door closed behind him, Ian couldn't suppress a small smile before turning back to his work.

"A true Volsung all right," he mused out loud. Proud and stubborn. Calculating but bold. Alan really did have Tristan's eyes.

"Are you planning on making my life as difficult as he did?"

Operation 7: The Escape

"You're slow, Jiordson," Alan said as the ringing of blades faded. Drachewunden rested between Alan and Sven's practice weapon. Though the practice blade had bend similar to Sven's rapier, the angle of Drachewunden prevented the tip from reaching Alan. "A sabre like Drachewunden shouldn't match the speed of your lunges. Your feints are too large — you need to tighten them up."

Alan gave Sven's sword a chastising *clink* before dropping the tip of his blade. Only after Sven lowered his weapon did Alan pull off his helmet. Sven panted from his exertion, and though Alan hadn't moved as much as his fencing partner, the heavy padding of the practice gear had worked up his own sweat. Alan was happy to set aside the helmet to feel the cool breeze of the garden's circulation system on the back of his neck as he stripped off the jacket and heavy sleeve.

"You're done already?" Sven whined. "But I wanted to spar after drills."

"Have you noticed that you don't have either an extra practice weapon, or an extra set of gear?" Alan gave Sven a withering look. "You think Drachewunden is a toy? The only time I'd ever swing him at someone would be in actual combat. I'm happy to drill with you, but we don't spar until you find me a safer weapon."

"Such a gentleman."

"I'm just not blood-thirsty."

Sven set down his sword and flopped, face up, on the floor of the gardens. He stared at the domed ceiling panels. It was toward evening so the garden lights were dimmed, and while the panels were just a little clouded, Alan could imagine the sea of stars shining beyond them.

"Nice evening, huh?"

Alan looked around, uncertain how Sven decided whether the Swallow's imitation day/night cycle constituted "nice."

"I...suppose it's at least as nice as the others."

They'd started fencing lessons after the incident with the Popinjay. Sven never bothered to hide his fascination with Drachewunden, and given that they'd built up quite a bit of trust during their mutual near-death experiences, it wasn't a complete surprise when Sven asked Alan to demonstrate some techniques with the famous blade. These demonstrations had progressed into Sven showing Alan his rapier, and from there, Alan found himself giving Sven private lessons once an evening.

All this was fine by Alan. It normalized the idea of arming Alan, as if he were a harmless pet under Sven's control, and, selfishly, Alan enjoyed fencing. It had been his hobby throughout his childhood and into the Academy, and he'd pursued it even after graduation.

With no false modesty, Alan was a very good fencer and had been since his youth. There was a reason his grandmother entrusted Drachewunden to him and not his other siblings, even if Alicia was the better fighter. Without question she was more skilled at combat, but she was not the better fencer.

Despite Alan being critical of Sven during their lessons, he could admit Sven was skilled enough to make the practice fun. Sven was a quick study. He picked up new techniques and adopted the adjustments Alan presented him despite a gap in experience.

"These gardens are beautiful," Sven murmured in a sentimental tone, returning Alan's thoughts to the present. "Bet your ships have nothing like them."

"That's true," Alan admitted as he seated himself beside Sven. "They are both impressive and pragmatic." After a moment he added, "And yes, beautiful."

The aquaponic gardens were all of these things. The pyreans had created numerous technological wonders for space travel, but their gardening and bioengineering were what made extended, nomadic life in space possible. These gardens also made the indefinite time spent traveling on a starship bearable. When Alan worked on human ships, the unending gray and white of the walls grew oppressive after a couple months. The sight of so much green and the smell of the water, even if it was slightly musty as though from a swamp, revitalized Alan in a way he hadn't imagined possible. It made the vast, indifferent maw of space feel almost cozy.

Sven yawned, folding his hands behind his head as his eyes slid shut. "I should go collect Eric soon. The provisioning team always yells at me if he snacks too much on the foliage."

"I can't imagine why."

Sven said nothing. After a pause, he murmured, "It's not so bad here, right, Alan?"

Alan stiffened. He could sense the trap, even if he couldn't quite understand the how or the why of it. But Alan didn't doubt it had something to do either with his new level of clearance, the negotiations with the HIA, or both.

Alan wasn't ready to mention his sudden, unexpected clearance to Sven. If Sven was playing a game, he wouldn't tell Alan anyway, and on the off-chance it was a fluke or accident, Alan didn't want to ruin his advantage. Instead he asked the question he asked at least once a day.

"Jiordson, how are the negotiations for my release proceeding?"

"These things take time. You know how it goes." It was the typical non-answer Alan had grown used to hearing. Sven opened one eye. "I know you're a hostage. There's no pretending otherwise, but that's not all you are to me — to us. I want you to be happy. You can still have fun here, can't you?"

Fun...

Alan's first instinct was to deny any sort of imprisonment could be fun, but if he were honest, he was having fun. The longer he was here, especially with the increased freedom he'd been given this past week, the more it felt like a bizarre cruise vacation rather than a hostage situation. Yet that was precisely the reason why he needed to escape as soon as possible.

"Fun or no, a cage is a cage, Captain," Alan replied in a soft voice. He crossed his legs and gazed across the gardens. "You of all people must understand that."

When Sven said nothing, Alan eyed Sven through his bangs. "And what I am to you? Great-grandson of Tristan von Volsung? The direct descendant of a pirate legend? If I asked for a place on this ship, would you take me for that reason alone?"

Sven sat up, leaning on his elbows. He looked at Alan with an earnest, hopeful expression. "Not for that reason alone, but of course. You may be part human, but you're still one of us. You have the heart of a star sailor, Alan — a pyrean's heart."

Alan paused. When he spoke, it was in a low, serious voice. "And if I asked you to let me go?"

Sven's eyes widened with obvious hurt and disappointment, but Alan felt only a little bad. Alan had set the trap, yes, but he was an actual prisoner here.

Sven rose to his feet and sheathed his rapier. "When my superiors say to release you, I certainly will." As he dusted off his pants, he added, "I need to find Eric."

When Alan rose to follow him, Sven waved a hand. "I'll be

fine on my own. Do as you please, Inspector. You're our guest until the IPC and HIA reach an accord."

Alan stared, not quite sure if he should believe what was happening. Sven had left him alone and armed. It was either the captain's most extreme act of carelessness, or this was the final bait. Alan didn't doubt he'd hurt Sven's feelings — Sven wore his heart on his sleeve too much to fake that — but that didn't make him any less canny.

But bait or no, this was the best chance Alan would get. He sheathed Drachewunden and grabbed his coat, leaving the gardens and his padded practice gear behind him.

SCENARIO AFTER SCENARIO played through Alan's head as he walked toward the communications room. There was always a skeleton crew on duty through the night, but most of the ship members would be off shift, drinking and playing games in the mess hall as part of their evening ritual. Thus the hallways were quiet but not empty. Alan maintained a purposeful stride, ignoring the crew mates he passed in the same way he'd ignored them since starting his walks. The hardest part was not fiddling with Drachewunden. The fact that he was armed should have been a concern, but trying to hide the weapon any more than draping his coat over the arm that held it would only call more attention to it. Yet none of the crew members Alan passed paid him any heed.

When he reached the communications room, he raised a hand to palm open the door, only to hesitate when he heard voices within. The voices were hard to distinguish with the door muffling the sounds, but one of them he recognized as Ragnar's. He'd met the Communication Officer by chance once, and Alan had been interested in him since. The other was a woman's voice, but it was too soft to identify.

One person he'd expected. Two people was a problem.

Yet the Fates were on Alan's side this once. As the conversation continued, it became clear that Ragnar was chatting with the woman through the long range comm system. A social call from the sound of it. Like humans, pyreans used a quantum lattice to allow for instantaneous communication across the galaxy. Communication, unlike travel, was cheap and fast, but human vessels, especially Elite ones, had strict rules about personal versus professional use. It shouldn't have been a surprise that the Pyrean Navy was more lax.

"Babe, I gotta go, but I have shore leave saved up, and I was gonna burn it during our scheduled maintenance on Psyche. Why don't we meet up there? I'll get you the deets."

The woman said something too muffled to hear through the door, but the answer seemed to please Ragnar. "Absolutely! See you then. Love ya!"

As Ragnar ended his call, Alan made his move. He opened the door and quickly assessed the situation. As he'd hoped, Ragnar was alone. An empty communications room was great, but one with an expert user of the system was even better. Ragnar was in the middle of stretching as he got out of his seat when he noticed Alan.

"What...?"

Alan dashed forward and drew his sword. In one swing he laid the blade on Ragnar's throat.

"Say nothing."

Ragnar complied, but his eyes darted between the sword's blade and Alan's face, as though to determine how serious the human was.

"I will bring no harm to this vessel, you have my word," Alan said. "But I do not guarantee your personal safety if you try something heroic."

"Oh, don't worry about that," Ragnar replied with a nervous laugh. "I'm happy to live a cowardly, easy-going life."

"Then we'll get along just fine," Alan assured him. "I'll tell you the channel and the message I want you to send."

"I won't be able to encrypt it unless you share a key."

"Encryption is not necessary."

Ragnar nodded. "May I take a seat?"

"Yes, but I will know if you type anything more than my request."

"You're the boss!"

Ragnar did as he was told. Alan dictated what to send, and at no point did Ragnar try to turn on his comm or send any additional messages. Once Ragnar finished, Alan nodded, pulling the sword enough off of the man's neck that Ragnar could move away from the keyboard.

"Apologies, but I'll need to take your comm and secure you for the time being. After that, we will hopefully not inconvenience each other again."

Ragnar nodded. As Alan bound him with some cabling cords pulled from one of the utility trunks, Ragnar admitted, "You humans really are so polite. Makes me kinda feel bad for always stealing from you."

Alan hauled Ragnar into the small closet and gagged him. "You know, I think that's the nicest thing a pirate has ever said to me."

After closing the closet door, Alan retrieved Drachewunden and proceeded to the emergency escape pods.

Colony 23.401 was a pyrean port orbiting the mixed planet, 25TR-23. Gating from Earth to here would take time, but if Colin had his wits about him, he'd be able to decipher Alan's message and call in support from the nearby human colonies. All that was left was for Alan to deactivate an escape pod's tracking device and ride it to the planet's surface.

There were numerous emergency pods scattered across the ship, but he'd already decided on one of the single-person pods in a quieter side bay. Smaller pods had less tracking capability than the big ones, so it would take less time to disable. Even with Ragnar secured, Alan doubted he had more than twenty minutes, and that was generous.

Fortunately this particular bay was empty at this time of night. Alan opened one of the pods and took a seat before pulling out the tools he'd appropriated from Dirk's tool kit. He didn't work as fast as he had hoped, but it was fast enough. After clipping the last of the wires connecting the tracker, he reached down to begin the launch sequence. A gun cocked from behind him.

Alan froze. His hand was just a couple palm lengths from the hatch controls. If he was fast enough to hit the button...

"I wouldn't try it," Sven murmured as though reading Alan's thoughts. "Hatch doors close kinda slowly, and we already established I can pry them open if I feel like it. Which I probably will."

It was true. Alan's best bet would be to subdue Sven and then escape the ship. He raised his hands in surrender before turning to better assess the situation. Sven was alone. Whether it was a stroke of luck or Sven's overconfidence, Alan didn't know or care. It worked in his favor either way. If he could get close enough to disarm Sven, escape would still be possible.

"Well, here we are," Alan murmured. "I don't suppose you'll finally tell me what the IPC and HIA decided."

Sven cocked his head but kept the gun pointed at Alan. "I think you can guess."

Alan sighed. Indeed he could. He'd had his suspicions for a while, but it was nice of Sven to point a gun at him to make the situation crystal clear.

"So you gave me higher level clearance to what? See how I'd react? Give yourself some entertainment before you shipped me off to a naval prison?"

"You were going to figure out sooner or later that the HIA wouldn't negotiate your release," Sven answered with a shrug. "I figured I might as well tempt you into an escape attempt before then. Before you got desperate and did something we'd all regret."

"Why?" Alan hissed with sudden frustration. "To put me in my place? To make it clear you're my master, and I never stood a chance?"

Sven gave Alan a look of exasperation. "Well that's a lot of intent being read into my actions. No, Alan. I was just buying myself some time. I had a plan, you know."

When Alan just looked at him in confusion, Sven flipped on the safety and lowered the gun. He placed it on the ground and knocked it with the side of his foot, sending it spinning into a dark corner of the hangar.

"But plans change."

Alan only noticed Sven's rapier sheathed at his side when Sven started to draw it, leveling the tip at Alan's chest.

"How about a wager?" Sven said with a sharp look. "First one to draw blood wins. If you win, you get to leave on that escape pod. No one tries to follow you. No one tells the IPC you're gone until we confirm the Elite has picked you up."

Alan's eyes narrowed. It was too good to be true. Unquestionably a trap. Yet Alan's fingers itched to reach for his own blade.

"And if you win?"

Sven grinned a wicked, knowing grin. A devil indeed. "You give me your word on your family's honor that you will not try to escape or contact any human authority until I give you permission to do so."

Alan's eyes narrowed. "Which family?"

Sven's eyes flashed with amusement. "Volsung, Beringer. Whatever you choose to call yourself, why should I doubt your word of honor?" He raised his sword in a salute. "Well? What will it be, Inspector?"

"I..." Alan hesitated.

His mind whirred through the possible outcomes, weighing the risks and rewards, gauging the traps within traps. But ultimately it was a simple proposal. Alan wondered if Sven somehow knew how irresistible of a proposal it would be to Alan.

He drew Drachewunden, leveling the blade at Sven's chest.

"It's unfair," Alan declared. "All the risk is on me — not you. How about a change to make it more interesting?"

"Oh?" Sven's eyes lit up with curiosity. Wagers were irresistible to star sailors, especially pyrean ones, and the higher the stakes, the better.

"If I win, you allow me to escape to the planet. And I get to keep you as my hostage."

Rather than respond, Sven just blinked as if taken aback. He considered the addendum for a long moment, before bursting into laughter. Sven dropped the tip of the blade, yet his green eyes bored into Alan with sharp ferocity.

"That will make things much more interesting, won't it?" Sven murmured. "Spirits, Alan, you're truly wasted on the Elite, you know that? But all right, I agree to your terms. Do we have ourselves a wager?"

Alan nodded. "I accept."

OPERATION 8: THE DUEL

"I accept," Alan repeated. "But I want to make one thing clear, Captain."

When Sven cocked his head, Alan tilted Drachewunden, drawing a gleam from the black blade despite the dim lighting. Everything about his sword was thicker and heavier than Sven's whip-light rapier.

"Drachewunden is not a dueling weapon. I told you that if I draw him, it means I'll fight as though it's actual combat. You will be trying to draw blood. I'll be trying to kill."

Sven's eyes widened, and for an instant Alan wondered if he'd withdraw his challenge. But then Sven smiled, teeth forming a sharp predatory grin of anticipation. There was no fear, Alan realized. Only excitement.

"I want you, Alan." Something about the way Sven said those words made Alan's stomach flutter. The sensation wasn't quite fear or unease, but it traveled through his gut and into his chest. Alan's heart hammered in his ears. "It's only fair that I should put my own life on the line, yeah?"

"Hn." Alan adjusted his grip on Drachewunden. "Just don't blame me when you need to replace a whole limb this time."

With a laugh, Sven gave Alan one last salute before raising his blade.

"En garde," he said in flawless French.

Alan took his stance as well. "Oui."

They waited, blades just out of striking range.

"Fence," Sven said.

He was being a gentleman, Alan realized. Sven waited an extra beat to give Alan time before moving in. This was to be a clean fight, then — something Alan hadn't counted on.

Sven came in fast and low, as was his habit, so Alan had no trouble parrying the probing lunge. Before Alan could riposte, Sven darted out to the side to continue fishing for Alan's weak points.

A sabre versus a rapier was an unorthodox match to say the least. Sabres were designed for slashing — strong, heavy blades for cutting swathes of enemies — while rapiers were piercing — fast, flexible blades for penetrating armor. Rapiers were considered the superior choice in dueling, and even more so in this scenario where a single scratch that drew blood constituted victory. Additionally Sven fenced left-handed. Since most humans were right-handed, it provided an advantage in fencing, as it did in boxing and other sports, where a left-handed combatant had more experience with right-handed opponents than vice versa.

No doubt these factors contributed to Sven's confidence, even if Alan had more training and overall better technique. But at the end of the day, it wasn't the blade that mattered, or details related to form and rules, so much as the fighter. The sabre was not a weapon known for encouraging patience, but Alan's defense was solid enough he could take his time, waiting for the right moment to punish Sven's eager strikes.

The next round of exchanges continued in the same way. Sven would come in, Alan would push back Sven's advances, but neither Sven's tip would land nor could Alan get in a clean ripose. It was easy to overcommit in sabre, and he could tell Sven was trying to bait this out, yet Alan could see that, little by little, Sven was growing complacent. He'd fallen into this rhythm, and if Alan could remain sharp, Sven would be the one to overcommit.

Sven side-stepped into Alan's open line. His rapier raced toward Alan's flank, but when Alan angled his blade to parry it, Sven feinted, the tip of the rapier dipping under Alan's blade. Sven had finally committed, aiming for the underside of Alan's wrist in what would normally be an ideal trap. The delicate, whip-like blade of a rapier could dance around a sabre with ease, but Sven's feint was as sloppy now as it had been earlier this evening.

Alan had been waiting for this moment. He parried with prime, all but shoulder-checking Sven as he stepped forward for the riposte. He slashed the blade toward Sven's midsection. Upward of the waist was valid target in sports sabre, but he didn't need to aim too much in a live duel. A cut across the flank, hips, or thigh would each constitute a victory.

An instant later, Alan's blade connected, but his sense of victory was short-lived. Sven had caught Drachewunden with his right hand — the prosthetic hand — before it could cut into flesh. Alan realized what was happening a moment too late. Before he could react, Sven tightened his grip on Drachewunden's blade and yanked. Alan managed to hold onto his weapon, but he stumbled a step before regaining his balance.

As Alan tried to recover, Sven loosened his grip and stepped back. With a flick of his wrist, the rapier tip came down in a delicate, whip-like strike against Alan's shoulder. Warmth flooded the right side of his body followed a moment later by the sharp sting of pain. Yet Alan hardly noticed either sensation. His eyes were fixed on Sven's blade and the bright red drops that gleamed along the edge of the steel.

Sven's grin turned into a wince as he waving his mangled right hand, as if to make sure Alan could see it. "No blood, yeah? I win!"

Alan hadn't felt his grip loosen, but he heard Drachewunden hit the ground with a *clang*. A moment later, he followed his sabre to the floor. He could feel the blood dripping down his back and chest, but he didn't bother to staunch it.

"No..."

He should have known. He should have considered Sven's prosthetic in his calculations. His cheeks flushed with a fresh wave of humiliation — a sour note complementing the already bitter tang of defeat.

"You should get that shoulder looked at, Alan." Sven's tone was not unkind, but the cheery matter-of-factness fanned the ire smoldering in Alan's belly. He paused before continuing, talking as much to himself as Alan, "Guess we'll have to stay a couple extra days in port while I see if that medical engineer can fix this."

Sven inspected his mangled hand. It was less broken than the previous model had been, but it still looked painful — and expensive.

"That was dirty," Alan muttered.

"But within the rules," Sven agreed before tapping his chest with a smug look. "Pirate, remember?"

He wiggled the fingers of his prosthetic, one by one to check the mobility of each knuckle's servos. They seemed remarkably intact given the damage Drachewunden's blade had inflicted, but Sven grimaced in pain at the motions.

"So what now?" Alan asked, his eyes fixed on the ground before him. "I just wait on this ship while Elite agents search the area for me? You're not even going to bother to hide?"

"What should I be hiding, Alan?" Sven cocked his head as if surprised by Alan's suggestion. "Even if they realize you're on board the Swallow, what can they do? How long do you think it would take them to get a warrant for a Pyrean Navy vessel? Or are you planning on breaking your word and staging another escape?"

Alan felt his face flush with the utter humiliation of this situation. Sven couldn't have left Alan's pride more in tatters if he'd tried, yet Sven wasn't even trying. He didn't need to. The contempt he felt for the Elite, for Alan, was not even conscious. It didn't need to be. Alan was helpless on his own, but Colin and the others couldn't help him now. A wave of despair passed through Alan.

What am I going to do?

"Hey."

Alan looked up, starting a little. Sven had knelt in front of him, his left hand hovering over Alan's good shoulder as though he was considering giving Alan a reassuring pat. Fortunately for Alan, Sven thought better of this and withdrew the hand.

"Go to the med bay, okay?" Sven insisted. "If you want the room to yourself tonight, I'll find somewhere else to sleep."

"Do as you'd like, Jiordson," Alan hissed. He picked up Drachewunden and rose to his feet. His shoulder was starting to become distractingly painful, but Alan did his best to stand straight. "But yes, I'll escort myself to the medical bay. Have a good night."

THE MEDICAL BAY was empty this late in the evening, but Katja arrived soon after Alan let himself into the room. She yawned as she entered, her usual messy bun now a messy ponytail, and when she came closer, Alan noticed her shirt was inside out.

"I'm sorry," Alan said, realizing she must have rolled out of bed just for him. "I could have dressed it myself, but I didn't want to look around for supplies without your permission."

Katja gave him a sleepy wave. "I'd prefer to be woken up over rummaging. You probably can't tell by looking at me, but I'm very picky about organization." She eyed his bloody shoulder. "Let's see this injury then."

Alan protested when she started helping him out of his shirt, but by now his shoulder was both painful and stiff, and he needed the assistance. The good news was it wasn't a deep wound, so the bleeding had already stopped.

As Katja began to clean up the injury, she said, "Sven mentioned you had a shallow sword wound but not much else. I wasn't sure what to expect to be honest. He has a poor track record when it comes to his own injuries, but looks like he was correct when assessing someone else. Maybe Sven is a better swordsman than I give him credit for."

She swabbed the wound with a disinfectant, Alan doing his best not to flinch, before she began to bandage it up.

"Won't need stitches, but I want to check on it in a couple days to see how it's healing. I'd give you some painkillers, but let me do the pyrean-human conversions tomorrow when I'm less sleepy."

She tossed the bloody shirt into a wash bin by the door and wandered into her office. From the other room she called out, "I'll see if I can find a spare shirt in the meantime. Just a moment."

As Alan waited, his mind played through the duel. Every move, every decision. Every mistake.

Stupid, arrogant fool.

Alan closed his eyes and took a deep breath. He had no one to blame but himself, but even without self-recriminations, he felt lost.

What am I going to do now?

Katja returned with a spare shirt and an apologetic look. "I know it's too big, but it's all I have here. It should at least get you back to your quarters with fewer stares."

Alan eyed the garment. The shirt was made for someone with a larger frame than his own — an unfitted pullover with a wide collar and long sleeves. It was the exact style Alan avoided when dressing himself, but he couldn't afford to be picky. Alan pulled on the shirt, careful to mind his injured shoulder. The material was soft, but the sleeves were so long, they engulfed his hands. He felt a bit like a child trying on his parents' clothes.

"Um, actually..." Alan murmured as he fiddled with a sleeve.

"Is there any way I could sleep here? If you'd need to stay and watch over me, I'll leave, but I promise not to touch anything."

For a long moment, Katja considered this request. She regarded him with a look of scrutiny, as if trying to figure out what he wanted. On some level, Alan hoped Katja would assume he was too angry to spend the night in Sven's quarters, rather than the sad truth that he wasn't angry — he just wasn't ready for another round of humiliation facing Sven.

At last she nodded.

"Feel free to use a bed. You can grab some sheets from this bin. Daice will be here in the morning, but I'm going back to sleep."

Alan gave her a slight bow. "Thank you. I appreciate it, Officer Lang."

She laughed. "Officer Lang, huh? I haven't heard that in a while. It's just 'Katja' when I'm on the Swallow, lad." She palmed open the door, but before stepping through, she turned to regard Alan. "You're a good kid. Have a good night."

Alan opened his mouth in protest to being called a kid, but then he considered her three earring studs and realized she was likely quite a bit older than her appearance suggested.

"Good night, Katja," he replied.

When the door closed behind her, Alan got up to pull out a sheet and dim the lights. The medical bed was a strict downgrade from his bed in Sven's room, but between his aching shoulder and the unanswerable question of "what now? what now? what now?" Alan wouldn't have slept well anywhere.

***

ALAN WOKE from his restless slumber as the light clicked on. Daice entered the room. Alan managed to raise his head to regard the young medic, but his brain was too foggy to put together words, or understand what was happening.

"Oh, sorry!" Daice yelped. "Sorry, sorry. You can keep sleeping. I'm just gonna —" Daice gestured to the adjacent office before dimming the lights and scurrying inside.

Alan let his head flop back to the bed, but the sensation of sleepiness had started to fade, even if the grogginess hadn't. With a soft groan, he turned and immediately regretted it when his shoulder flared with pain. With effort and even more pain, Alan tried again. This time, he managed to sit up.

As he rubbed the sleep from his eyes, the med bay door opened a second time. The newcomer said nothing. Except for the sounds of booted feet stepping across the threshold, there was only silence.

Alan turned to face the door. Ian leaned against the wall with his arms crossed.

"Good morning, Beringer," Ian said at last.

Alan pinched the bridge of his nose. "You were in on it, I suppose."

"What? Giving you clearance in areas you shouldn't have clearance to tempt you into an escape? Of course. It was Sven's plan, but he needed some assistance. He's in the midst of some rather delicate negotiations, and the last thing he needs is an uncontrolled escape attempt where someone gets hurt."

With a bitter laugh, Alan shook his head. "So make sure it's a controlled escape attempt. Not bad thinking." He cradled his head in his hands. "And so you played me for a fool in the process."

"Oh please, Beringer," Ian said, uncrossing his arms with a sigh. "No self-pity. It doesn't suit you. You almost had it, you know. Especially when Sven decided to improvise with that foolish wager. When he told me what happened last night, I almost lost it."

Alan nodded. "He's not a bad fencer, but he's sloppy."

"Exactly."

Alan eye Ian. "Didn't stop him from winning."

Ian shrugged. "He may not be as good as you at fencing, but

he's an all-arounder when it comes to fighting. Sometimes that's enough."

"Noted," Alan acknowledged, a faint, self-deprecating smile flashing across his lips. "I suppose you can't tell me any more about these 'delicate negotiations' while you're here, though?"

Ian cocked his head. "You didn't actually think Sven would keep you here to himself forever?"

"The thought certainly crossed my mind," Alan retorted. He gave Ian a dubious look. "Jiordson really thinks he can come to an amiable agreement where IPC and HIA diplomats have failed?"

"Of course. Whether or not he succeeds, we'll have to wait and see."

Alan rose to his feet. Despite everything, he felt unexpected fondness rise up within him at the thought of Sven and whatever outlandish plan he was concocting. Sven's victory smarted, but Alan couldn't help some amount of grudging admiration for how well Sven had played him.

"I'd say I won't hold my breath, but Sven is in turns the most foolish of impulsive idiots and a cunning tactician, so I don't really know what to think."

Giving Alan a fond pat on his good shoulder, Ian said, "That's part of what makes him so dangerous, I reckon. Now. Let's get to the mess hall before breakfast runs out. You must be starving."

Alan's stomach grumbled in response. The walk from the med bay to the mess hall wasn't long, but from the way Ian talked about food running out, Alan had assumed they would miss the peak breakfast window. He felt a wave of surprise, and not a little anxiety, as the doors to the hall opened revealing rows of packed tables. Worse yet, the whole room went silent when the crew noticed Alan and Ian in the doorway. Alan felt his face flush under the scrutiny, but just as quickly as the chatter died down, it picked back up. All heads turned away from Alan to resume their conversations.

"What...exactly does the general crew know about my situation?"

"Oh, the broad strokes, you could say," Ian replied in the most unhelpful way possible. He gave Alan another gentle slap on the back. "All right, boyo. No need to be shy. Let's get you some grub."

Ian peered over the crew members in the hall before his eyes settled on a place in the corner. "Ah, Dirk and Lance are here."

As they approached the twins, Dirk gave Alan a cheerful wave. Alan flushed again as he remembered the tools he'd stolen from Dirk for his escape attempt.

"Don't worry," Ian murmured as if reading Alan's thoughts. "Sven returned the equipment you took after your duel, and Dirk's not the kind of lad to hold a grudge."

When they reached the table occupied by the twins, Ian gave them a commanding nod. "I see you're both done with your meals, boys. Be good lads and bring us some food too."

"Sir!" Lance acknowledged with a hasty salute. Dirk was about to say something to Alan, but Lance grabbed him by the wrist, pulling him toward the mess line.

Ian gave a fond chuckle as he took a spot on the long bench. "Now where were we, Beringer? Any more questions?"

Alan took a seat across from Ian before lacing his hands in front of him. "Many, but I suppose I'll focus on the immediate ones. Do I still have unrestricted access to the ship?"

"You're practically crew, aren't you?"

Alan winced at the implication, but nodded. "And Sven is having you babysit me?"

"Not exactly. I figured you could use some company after everything. Sven's back on the colony orbiting TR-23. He's looking into getting his hand fixed before we leave port, because if Admiral Jiordson finds out his son burned through two prosthetics in as many weeks, Sven might actually die."

Alan nodded, wondering just how in debt the prosthetic repairs would make Sven. It was petty, but knowing Sven's victory came at some price was better than believing it had been a complete defeat. "And Ragnar? You did find Ragnar, right?"

"I'm here!"

"Gah!"

Alan couldn't help jolting at the unexpected voice behind him. Ragnar continued to smile, a cup of coffee in one hand, as he gave Alan's injured side a friendly pat with his other hand. Alan tried not to wince.

"No hard feelings, though," Ragnar said as he took a seat next to Alan. "Definitely won't complain that Ian came to check on me not too long after you left. I was a bit worried I might have to spend the whole night bound and gagged in the closet."

"Er...I'm sorry about that."

"I just told ya no hard feelings!" Ragnar gave Alan a playful elbow in the injured arm (again), and Alan couldn't help wondering if maybe there were a few subconscious hard feelings. Ragnar continued, "Makes a great story, though. Dirk got a kick out of it when I told him this morning."

"Oh, you told Dirk?" Alan couldn't say why he felt so guilty about Dirk knowing the details of his attempted escape. Perhaps it was because he reminded Alan of Lyndas. As rarely as Alan visited the family estate, a pang of homesickness overcame him as he thought about his brother and sisters back on Earth.

"Look," Ragnar said, his jovial smile fading into a more sincere expression. "Everyone on board this ship takes their duty seriously. You did what you have to do. Dirk knows it, the captain knows it, and even I know it — though you probably think me a coward for letting you have your way."

Alan gave Ragnar a wry smile. "I'm just glad we avoided unnecessary heroics. I'm sure you would have stopped me if you thought I was putting the ship in danger."

"Yes, and I'd have hated every moment of it." Ragnar's cheerful grin made Alan laugh despite himself.

"Here's your grub, Chief," Lance said, placing a tray of food and a cup of coffee in front of Ian.

"And yours, Alan," Dirk added.

"Ah, thanks," Alan murmured, accepting the food and coffee with more enthusiasm than he wanted to admit.

As the twins took their seats across from Alan and Ian, Alan tried to eat with some decorum, but it was hard not to scarf it down. Perhaps it was just hunger but it tasted better than anything he'd eaten alone in Sven's cabin — no small feat considering how good all the food on board pyrean vessels tasted in comparison to the slop human ships served during interstellar journeys. Elite fare consisted of freeze-dried rations with little to no flavoring. Having fresh vegetables and spices in a ship meal was unheard of except on luxury cruises.

"So are you really gonna be staying with us?" Ragnar asked.

As if in response, the bite of food in Alan's mouth turned flavorless and chalky. He chewed slowly before forcing himself to swallow. Only after he'd set down his fork did Alan murmur, "I'm afraid so."

Ian said nothing, continuing to sip at his coffee, while Ragnar's face paled as though he realized he'd said something he shouldn't have. Dirk cut in, mentioning something with the intent of changing the subject, but Alan hardly listened. He could only think of his family back on Earth, and the human authorities of TR-23, who even now were searching the surface of the planet for a escape pod they would not find.

Sven wouldn't keep Alan here forever, Ian insisted. Yet with Sven so unforthcoming about Alan's situation or how he intended to resolve it, it was hard to imagine Sven would willingly yield the power he held over Alan.

Despite wave after wave of frustration and despair washing over him, Alan did his best to enjoy the rest of his meal and rejoin the conversation, but every bite of food was a fresh taste of ash in his mouth as he contemplated his future.

OPERATION 9: TURNABOUT

COLIN FELT the sensation of time stop as the ship deGated, but he didn't break his stride. As soon as the chime sounded, indicating they were back in relative space, he tapped his ear piece.

"Inspector Mitchell here. As soon as we dock on 23.22, please have the TR-23 team meet me in our briefing room."

"Yes, Sir."

It would be another twenty to thirty minutes to complete the vessel's docking procedures, but Colin wanted that time to prepare. Once in the briefing room, he connected his tablet to the main display and set out the loaner tablets for the TR-23 team.

Colin hated running meetings. When Alan wasn't busy being kidnapped by pirates, he was the one who took point on the meeting-related aspects of their duties. Colin missed Alan for other reasons, but never having to create a meeting agenda again was a key motivating factor in Colin's search for his partner.

As the ship began its docking procedures, Colin continued to scroll through his notes and documents without really seeing them. It had been five Earth days since the cryptic message had arrived from the vicinity of TR-23 on an Elite emergency channel. Colin had decided to look into it on a hunch, and his suspicions proved correct. The message was unencrypted, but he recognized one of the ciphers that Alan and he had created on an earlier mission.

Look for escape pod on TR-23.

Colin had immediately contacted the authorities on Colony 23.22, which orbited the planet, before catching the next available shuttle off Earth and toward the 25TR system. Even a small pyrean vessel's Gate engines could warp longer distances than fixed-point human Gates could, so Colin had used the past four days of travel to study every piece of evidence, even if the local team's planetwide searches had been fruitless thus far.

When his ensign reported the TR-23 team had boarded and was heading his way, Colin set down his tablet with a sigh. He made a half-hearted effort to pat down his thick, rumpled hair, but he already knew that was a hopeless battle. Colin only bothered to get a haircut twice a year for his semi-annual reviews, but his hair's natural inclination was to form spiky cowlicks that only an obscene amount of gel could keep at bay. There was no way he was going to look the part of a well put together Elite Inspector.

It occurred to Colin that he'd come to rely on Alan, with his gentleman's manners and handsome appearance, to set a good impression with their local support teams. Colin wasn't ill-mannered per se, nor was he bad-looking, but he couldn't quite captivate a room quite like Beringer could.

The TR team filed into the meeting room behind Colin's ensign, and Colin greeted them one by one. Between Colin's Gate hops, they'd been in frequent communication these past few days, but this was the first time meeting them in person.

"Thank you for coming," Colin said with a pleasant half-smile. "I certainly appreciate your assistance on this investigation, even if progress has been slow."

The head of the TR team, Major Amaechi, nodded in acknowledgement, but her expression remained serious. In their previous communications, she'd been communicative and committed to the task at hand, but she made no attempt at pleasantries, nor did she have any interest in building relations between her team and Colin's beyond what was necessary.

This wasn't unusual. Most local police bodies preferred to avoid Elite interference as the Elite both had the authority to take over these sorts of investigations and invoked this power frequently. In some ways, the Elite garnered more respect from pyrean organizations than they did from the human systems.

"We've initiated searches near our on-planet settlements," Major Amaechi said, pulling up satellite images of the planet. "At this point, we've scanned every meter of the planet with our satellites. We're not finding anything. Our analysts are in the process of reviewing all energy readings from orbiting vessels from the past six days, but that will take longer to complete. That said, we haven't detected any undocumented launches from any of them. If Inspector Beringer did manage to escape his captor's ship, we're having a hellava time finding any trace of this."

Colin's polite smile turned a little wry. "While I'll certainly want to review those records on the off-chance that dear Beringer is unusually stealthy, the reasonable assumption is that his escape attempt failed, and he remains a captive. Since the IPC has not issued any statements about Inspector Beringer's status, it's also safe to assume he is alive and mostly unharmed from the incident."

"Then the ship he's on has probably left this system, Inspector Mitchell," Major Amaechi replied. "We've checked public docking records across all colonies, including the two pyrean-controlled ones. All pyrean vessels that were docked here five days ago have left by now."

Major Amaechi's calm, professional expression flashed with frustration for just an instant, mirroring Colin's own feelings. The authorities on Colony 22 had no ability to hold ships docked on other colonies, and certainly not the pyrean ones. Even if Colin somehow had arrived sooner, there was no way a pyrean vessel would allow the Elite to board without an HIA warrant, which was the type of warrant that required evidence beyond mere probable cause. Everything about the situation was in the kidnappers' favor, and both the kidnappers and the investigative authorities knew this.

"Yes, I read that report before this last Gate hop," Colin said with a helpless shrug. "It is what it is. I wasn't expecting anyone involved to stick around very long, so that's not unexpected. The good news is, I have a pretty good guess as to which vessel Alan sent that message from."

"Oh?" Major Amaechi cocked an eyebrow. Her cool expression flickered with a spark of interest, as though Colin had finally managed to impress her. Colin couldn't quite hide a self-satisfied smirk. He enjoyed impressing people — being appreciated — and Major Amaechi was an attractive woman on top of this. Even if he wasn't quite enough of a scoundrel to outright flirt with a coworker — particularly when his partner was being held captive by pirates — he could at least enjoy impressing her.

"It's taken a while to get meaningful data from the signal analysis, but I noticed something interesting right before our vessel deGated." With the rest of the room waiting for an explanation, Colin continued, "After cross-referencing the message's signal with all other signals you've provided me from the past five days, there's a high probability the vessel was some type of schooner."

Colin scrolled through his notes to project the results of his analysis on the conference room's display. The math he'd used to get these results was relatively esoteric even in data analyst circles, but he had the details on hand should someone on the local team wish to see his methodology.

When no one did, Colin continued, "We already know the ship that abducted Alan was a Swallowtail, which is type of schooner. This suggests the abductors may not have transferred him as we originally assumed."

Colin highlighted a couple more dossiers of information for them to look through before folding his arms. "I had a chance to check every port's records across all TR-23 colonies. Only one Swallowtail was in orbit at the time the signal was sent."

Amaechi and several others on her team started examining the intel on their loaner tablets, but Colin pulled up the ship's information on the large screen behind him. "Swallowtail Class C Model 00489. She's part of the Pyrean Navy under the command of Captain Sven Jiordson."

"Is this captain a relation to Admiral Jiordson?"

"It's not an uncommon pyrean surname," Colin admitted. "But given everything, I think it's safe to assume our captain could be from a pirate family, and the Swallow could be part of the Navy's Piracy Division."

"She left just yesterday," Major Amaechi said after checking her records. "She was moored off of Colony 401." She shook her head in irritation. "It was an obvious vessel to investigate. I should have requested permission to board."

"And permission would have been denied," Colin countered. "Even if they had nothing to hide, Navy vessels are under no obligation to cooperate with us except in the face of overwhelming evidence. This way, at least, they aren't aware of how much we know, so they're less likely to transfer Inspector Beringer to a different vessel or secure him in a Navy prison. We're a few steps behind, but we're getting closer, Major."

"So what next?"

Colin ran a hand through his hair, but the gesture only made it messier. "I need your team to finish checking energy readings and then look into every schooner — whether or not they're flying pyrean flags — that has been in this system. What I have is a nice, clean working theory, but we can't afford to blind ourselves to other possibilities."

Major Amaechi nodded. "I agree, Inspector."

Colin scanned the other faces of the local authorities. "Are there any other thoughts or suggestions from the rest of the team? Please bring up anything interesting you noticed or observed no matter how trivial it may seem."

After a moment of consideration, the rest of the TR-23 team shook their heads. As Colin knew, most of the leads they'd been following prior to his arrival had run dry by now. Sorting through this data would keep them busy for the next few days, but as tedious as these tasks were, they seemed eager to get started on fresh theories.

Collecting his tablet, Colin rose from his seat before giving them a small bow.

"In that case, with your permission, Major, I'd like to join your team on Colony 22. I'll begin by assessing what records I can find on the Merry Swallow, and with any luck, we may be able to determine where they're going next."

The Major nodded, giving him a slightly more warm smile than she had at the start of the briefing. Colin returned the look, letting her know her interest had not gone unnoticed, before turning back to the holographic map of this sector, which was projected above the center of the conference table. The other members of the team filed out of the room, but Colin continued to stare at the geography of this system as though it might help him predict where the Swallow would go next.

Pyrean ships moved fast — far faster than humans could hope to match. In terms of raw speed and sheer force, the Elite stood no chance of seizing vessels. Yet the Elite's track record was a testament to how well their methods worked.

Patience. Deliberation. Slow, dogged persistence.

These methods had led to a number of unsavory nicknames that pyrean sailors called the Elite, yet each pyrean curse and slur was a point of pride to an Elite investigator — and Colin considered himself among the best of what the Elite could offer.

"Hurry up and escape, Alan," Colin murmured with a sly grin. "You know I'll never let you live it down if I rescue you first."

ALAN RECLINED ON HIS BED, reading through a pyrean history book. He was alone in Sven's quarters — his quarters now. In the handful of days since his defeat, he still couldn't quite accept that this was his new home — that only on the whims of Sven and the IPC could Alan hope to return to human space. Yet his initial feelings of despair had begun to pass. If anything, he'd been given more freedom since the duel, and except for the fact that Alan had no duties on board the ship and that the rest of the crew was pyrean, it was easy to imagine this was just another sailing excursion.

The embers of Alan's earlier humiliation had died into low-level melancholy. He wasn't unhappy, but he was dissatisfied in a way that had become more tangible since Sven extracted the promise on his honor. Before that promise, Alan had been working toward a goal, however roundabout the process. Now...

Alan sighed.

He needed a job. He set aside the book when he realized he hadn't paid attention to any of the words for the past several pages. Alan flopped back on his bed and stared up at the ceiling, hands folded behind his head. With all this spare time, he could probably learn another language. Brush up on his math and engineering skills. Maybe get a doctorate or two.

A human doctorate or a pyrean one? I'd need a remote program for the human one...how do doctorates work in pyrean universities?

This idle speculation, born from deep-seated ennui and boredom, was interrupted by a beep from Sven's comm. Sven was not here, but his comm was. Alan didn't need to be a detective to notice how often Sven forgot his comm, but Alan couldn't decide if it was extreme disorganization and flightiness, or if Sven just liked being left alone when he was off-duty. Possibly a combination of both.

Alan ignored the comm's beeps for some time, but at last, the person on the other end used the bypass to speak directly to the room.

"I know you're there, Beringer, and I know Sven ain't, so just pick up already."

Alan blinked at the sound of First Mate Segel's voice. Alan had only met Valtra a couple times and each encounter had been brief. They'd passed each other once in the hallway before the duel, and once since, and while Valtra had warmed up to him quite a bit since the first time, she remained distrustful. It was oddly refreshing to have at least one of his captors treat him like an actual threat rather than the ship mascot.

He picked up the comm. "This is Inspector Beringer. How can I help you, First Mate?"

"We got an incoming call for ya. From the Elite. I assume you'll want to take it."

"Yes!" Alan said with more intensity than he felt comfortable expressing. "Er...yes, please, Ms. Segel."

"Ragnar will redirect the call to Sven's terminal. It should go without saying that the communication is open, and we are monitoring it."

"Naturally. Thank you, First Mate."

"And enough with the 'Ms. Segel' and 'First Mate' already," Valtra added with a grumble. "Just call me Valtra like everyone else."

"My apologies, Valtra."

Alan heard a muttered "too bloody polite" before the line cut out, and the terminal display turned on.

Moments later, static appeared on the screen before resolving into a clear, high-resolution image. Alan's eyes widened.

"Chief Inspector!" Alan rose to give a formal salute. "My apologies, Chief Inspector, that I was unable to get into contact with you sooner."

The woman on the screen was older, her gray hair and hard craggy face reflecting both her age and fearsome dedication to her job. Her eyes were still sharp, though, and she regarded Alan with a raptor's gaze.

"No need for apologies, Inspector Beringer. We owe you the

apology for taking so long." She laced her fingers in front of her. "Inspector Mitchell received your transmission, by the way. I'm sure with a little more time he would have retrieved you himself."

Alan furrowed his brow. "A little more time?" he asked in confusion. "What do you mean, Chief Inspector?"

She leaned back in her seat before saying, "The situation has changed. I am contacting you on behalf of the HIA. I suspect the crew of the Merry Swallow is receiving a similar communication from the IPC, given that they're letting me speak to you."

Alan leaned forward, heart pounding. Sven had said the negotiations had broken down, and that the HIA was unwilling to give into demands, but something must have changed. "So the IPC and HIA have reached an agreement? I'll be freed soon?"

"Yes and no."

Alan's heart pounded harder, but this time will trepidation.

The Chief Inspector continued, "Yes, an agreement has been reached, and technically speaking they are ready to free you."

"But...?" Alan cut in, unable to stop himself.

"But," she agreed, "part of the arrangement is the creation of a new position within the Elite: Attaché Inspector of Observation. This position will exist to promote cross-species exchange and foster better cooperation and understanding between humans and pyreans. And this position is only available to you, Alan."

Alan froze, unable to parse so much new, unexpected information. Each of the title's words he understood, but put together...

"Chief Inspector," Alan mumbled with a shake of his head. "Forgive me if I'm being daft, and all of this is obvious, but am I to understand that you are giving me a new title, then leaving me on the Merry Swallow to observe a pyrean naval vessel, which is most certainly part of the Piracy Division, and this is something that both the IPC and HIA agreed to?"

The Chief Inspector sighed. "It's the ideal solution to everyone's problems, Alan." She gave him a pointed look. "You being the problem. The IPC no longer has to deal with an ongoing hostage situation, and the HIA saves face. The Elite get levels of access to the Pyrean Navy that has hitherto been impossible."

"And what does the Pyrean Navy get?"

She regarded him for a long, hard moment. "They get back one of their own."

Alan tried to hide his wince, but the Chief Inspector must have noticed. Her face softened. "That is not how the Elite sees you, of course. You are one of our top inspectors. You are a talented patriot, and no one here questions your loyalty. But the pyreans have a different perspective."

"Because of Tristan von Volsung." Alan was sick of saying that name.

"Yes," she agreed, much to Alan's chagrin. "My understanding is that he became personally involved in the negotiations, which probably hastened them on the IPC's side of things. And this means everyone is quite happy and ready to proceed with this exchange." When Alan said nothing, she added, "Except for you, Inspector Beringer. I already told the HIA that if you refuse this position, you will have the Elite's full support. I am hopeful HIA diplomats will reach a compromise that has you coming home even if you do not wish to go forward with this arrangement."

"But it's not a guarantee," Alan said.

"No," she admitted. "There is no guarantee. And there's no guarantee Colin will be able to extract you either."

Alan hesitated. "And it would be a pain for you and the Elite Agency if I were to refuse."

"Unquestionably." The Chief Inspector flashed a grim smile. "But everything about this situation is a pain. The choice is yours, Inspector. I don't want you to make this choice as a response to the political landscape. This is a request that comes with sacrifice and commitment, Inspector Beringer, and I know how practical you are, even when you shouldn't be. Therefore I am ordering you to consider this from the perspective of what you want personally — not deciding what's best for the HIA or the Elite."

"Chief Inspector —" Alan tried to interject, but the Chief Inspector continued before he could interrupt.

"Inspector Beringer, do you want to stay on the Swallow in a professional capacity, or do you want the HIA to try harder to get you home?"

Alan opened his mouth to protest, but he already knew it was useless. He closed his mouth with a sigh, at last managing a small smile. He was amused at how well the Chief Inspector knew him, and more than a little heart-warmed how much she cared about him.

Yet this time, there was no hard choice at all. As much as Alan hated being a captive, he did not hate this ship. He did not hate the Swallow's crew. He did not mind waiting a bit longer on those doctorates.

Alan asked, "Does this position come with a pay raise and additional shore leave?"

Operation 10: Fair Play

Once the conversation with the Chief Inspector concluded, Alan took a moment to stretch before rising from his seat. Dinner time was approaching, but Alan wasn't ready to face a crowd in the mess hall quite yet. Instead he left his quarters and made his way toward the gardens.

When the doors to the gardens opened, the scent of damp vegetation and a gentle, earthy breeze greeted him. Alan let his feet wander as he took in the verdant greens and mossy browns of the plants and ponds. Little by little he began to process the situation. Everything about the past month felt surreal and improbable, and the Chief Inspector's offer did nothing to lessen that sensation.

Yes, it had been an easy choice, but that didn't make it any less bizarre.

Alan had come to contemplate his situation in solitude, but he wasn't entirely surprised to hear sounds of other visitors further ahead. On a whim, he followed the noises, which came from the usual fencing spot he and Sven used. Even before Alan got close enough to see around the bend, he recognized the sounds of Sven practicing.

It had been a stroke of good luck for Sven that the medical engineer on Colony 401 was able to fix the mechanical parts of

Sven's prosthetic within TR-23's local week. That said, most of the damage was to the synthetic nervous system rather than the mechanical parts, and that would have to "heal" on its own. It would take time before full feeling would return to Sven's hand, and even then, there was a chance that the synthetic nervous system would not fully repair the damage. The doctor could not do anything about that without a full replacement, though. This early, there was no way to know, and the hand was in good enough condition to function with ongoing maintenance either way.

Yet these sorts of repairs did not come cheap, even for a naval captain. Sven had not told Alan how much it cost (on top of the full hand replacement he'd required not two weeks earlier), because every time Alan brought it up, Sven went into dramatic fits — bursts of melodrama that involved everything short of rolling on the floor and sobbing. When Alan had inquired with Ian and Dirk, Ian shook his head, calling Sven an idiot, while Dirk just laughed nervously and said it was good that basic living expenses were covered on the Swallow.

Yet that had not stopped Sven from returning to his fencing practice as soon as he was able. His back was to Alan as he practiced a set of lunging feints. Sven's form was getting better now that Alan insisted he practice drills regularly, but his talents had always laid in his quick decision-making and excellent situational awareness more than his fundamentals. He was a swashbuckler rather than a fencer, but as a point of personal pride after Alan's loss, Alan had decided to make Sven both of these things.

"Better, Jiordson, but you become sloppier as you get tired." Alan strolled toward Sven, who looked over with a start.

"Huh? Alan? Sorry, I didn't realize —"

Alan ignored Sven's rambling and grabbed his wrist. "You're angling the blade up too much when you reset. That's just asking to get your hand skewered. Even if you're drilling a particular action, you should maintain good form in between."

"Aye-aye," Sven replied with a soft, amused smile. He resumed his drills while Alan continued to inspect his form.

"Good. Much better. Next practice switching between the dueling and sport stance. Each makes different assumptions about the battlefield, but it's good to master both depending on the needs of the situation."

After watching a few more rounds of lunges, Alan mused, "Attaché Inspector of Observation, huh? Was that your plan all along?"

Sven flashed a grin, dropping his blade's tip as he regarded Alan with amusement. "Is that the title they decided on? It has a nice ring to it. Sounds like a promotion to me."

"Indeed," Alan nodded. "It comes with a very nice pay raise and extended vacation package."

"Um, you're welcome?"

"I'm not quite ready to thank you." Alan folded his arms. "Were you the one that brought my great grandfather into this?"

Sven's shoulders gave a guilty start before slumping. "I doubt the IPC would have agreed to the conditions without his insistence."

Alan peered at Sven with a considering look. "For someone who acts so easy-going, you have a knack for forcing other people's hands."

Sven dropped his eyes, choosing to examine the edge of his rapier rather than maintain Alan's gaze. "I suppose that goes with the whole 'pirate' territory. But I've been thinking, Alan. Right before our duel, you wanted to know what I'd do if you asked me to let you go. Remember?"

When Sven met Alan's eyes, uncertainty and open vulnerability made the pyrean look younger than his already youthful features suggested. Yet a hard light glinted in his eyes. Sven and Alan had known each other less than a month, but Alan could tell that Sven had come to some sort of decision.

"I remember," Alan replied.

"I will let you go if you want me to," Sven said. "I thought if you could still be with the Elite, if you weren't here as a hostage, you might want to stay. But this situation isn't fair, is it?" Sven tapped the tip of his blade on the ground in an absent gesture before continuing, "So if you decide to turn down the offer, if you truly want to leave, I will release you. I don't care what the IPC says or wants. I can't help it if a daring Elite inspector somehow manages to outwit me."

Alan cocked his head. "Daring, huh? While I am certainly interested to hear how this narrative would have played out, you should've told me sooner. I just accepted the offer."

Sven's face went pale before crumpling. "Alan, I...I —"

Taking an unusual amount of pity on the other man, Alan reached out to ruffle Sven's mess of hair. "I'm kidding, Jiordson. I did accept, but it wasn't because I was cornered into it." Alan cracked a dry smile. "For someone who likes toying with others, you're pretty easy to mess with."

A sudden urge to push aside Sven's mess of bangs overcame him, and Alan noticed his hand wandering to the side of Sven's face. He caught himself in time, forcing down the hand.

"I look forward to working with your crew as an official representative of the Elite," Alan continued. "Do watch what you say and do in front of me, though, because it is within my purview to document acts of piracy."

"Ah, the age old question," Sven murmured. "Is it piracy or a customs fee? I'll let our lawyers fight that one out."

"Fortunately I'm in investigation, apprehension, and now observation. None of which directly involve prosecution," Alan said. "Now why don't you finish those drills? Dinner just started, but you should end on a good note — make sure you keep up that form till the very end."

After a few more lunges, Sven paused, letting the tip of his blade drop. "Looking back, it was kinda stupid of me to challenge you to a duel, huh?"

Alan folded his arms. "You won, didn't you?"

Glancing in Alan's direction, Sven hesitated. "Yeah, but..."

"No buts," Alan cut in. "A loss is a loss. There is no 'I should have won' when it comes to combat. Certainly if you challenged me again, I would accept — fully believing in my victory — but that duel was yours. Losses teach us more than victories. I have no regrets."

Alan didn't put too much thought into his words as he said them, but from the way Sven stared at him, it seemed they resonated with the captain.

"Alan, you're so cool."

Sven spoke with such seriousness that it sounded facetious, but his eyes held genuine admiration. Alan felt himself flush, whether from the praise or because Sven was embarrassing, Alan couldn't say.

"And your form is still sloppy. Here." Alan put his hands on Sven's hips to adjust them. "Bend those knees. Loosen that shoulder. You're a natural fighter, why have such stiff posture all of the sudden? You need to relax."

"Like this, Alan?"

Sven leaned back against Alan, until Alan was partly supporting his weight. He looked up at Alan with a mischievous smirk, and Alan sighed, unsure whether to be exasperated or amused.

"When are you going to take this seriously, Jiordson?"

"Take what seriously?" A voice said from behind them. Then, "Oh."

Both Sven and Alan turned. Valtra stood by one of the pond tanks, arms crossed and face pinched in a look of long suffering.

"Sorry to interrupt," she said, giving them the sort of knowing look that made Alan's face heat despite himself.

He'd heard more than a few lewd remarks about Sven's "cabin boy" while walking the ship. Being partnered with Colin, who was something of a shameless scoundrel himself, had somewhat desensitized Alan to such quips, but Alan had grown up in polite society where those sorts of jokes were strictly off limits. He wasn't prepared or interested in dealing with them.

"Oh, you're not interrupting anything," Alan said stepping back from Sven on instinct. Sven hadn't caught his balance yet, so he crashed to the floor with a yelp. Alan winced in apology as Sven side-eyed him from the ground. "We're not...this isn't...this isn't what you think it is."

"So what do I think this is?" Valtra asked with a pointed stare.

"Something that's not what we're doing."

Sighing, Valtra shook her head, as if to tell Alan that she didn't know or care what he was up to, and she definitely didn't want any more information if she could help it.

"Regardless," Valtra said, changing the subject, "I need the capt to sign off on some books. Gunn wants to file them tonight, so the sooner the better. Would have just pinged you, Sven, but that would require you to, you know, have a comm on your person."

Sven looked sheepish as he picked himself off of the floor. "Oh yes, one of those. I must have dropped mine."

"It's in the room," Alan informed him.

"Oh, I guess it's in the room."

Valtra slung an arm around Sven shoulders and started dragging him toward the exit. Sven glanced back to wave at Alan. "Wanna meet up for dinner on the next bell?"

Alan gave a slight bow. "Very well, Captain Jiordson."

Sven turned back to Valtra as she began to overview the expenditure reports before they turned a corner, disappearing from view. Their voices grew faint and then went silent as the doors closed behind them, leaving Alan alone in the gardens.

As he looked across the pools and vegetation, the lights dimmed. The ship had begun to simulate night time. The clear dome above him grew transparent, allowing a multitude of stars to shine in from above. The delicate sounds of the water circulation system continued to tinkle around him.

Out of all the places in all of the galaxy Alan could be, Alan realized, the Merry Swallow wasn't so bad.

NATALIA HUMMED the tune of an old shanty as she strolled the corridor of the living quarters. Breakfast had ended a couple bells ago, but she snacked on a piece of fruit she'd grabbed on the way past the mess hall. Up ahead, a figure carrying a mop and bucket stepped out of the living quarter's head.

Valtra wore an expression of long suffering as she wiped her brow. Nat considered feeling sorry for her before deciding she was more pleased at having no chores for the next two weeks than she was sad on Valtra's behalf.

"Yo!" Natalia called out, taking another bite of her fruit. "I was wondering where you were all morning. I'm guessing Ian already came to collect?"

Valtra rested her elbow on the mop and leaned forward, heaving a sigh. Placing her other hand on her hip, she turned to glare at Natalia. "He cheated. The nerve of that man. He knew what Sven was plotting. I should have known he knew something, Ian acting so confident like that."

"What was it again?" Natalia mused, "Alan won't try to escape when Sven explains negotiations have broken down, right?"

"Yes," Valtra said in an unhappy voice. "And I was right. He did try to escape."

"But he tried to escape before Sven told him."

"That's what Ian says! Insists he won on a technicality. I said I won according to the spirit of the wager."

"And?" Natalia asked, knowing full well how this had ended.

"We made Gunnar break the tie, and he agreed with Ian. I should have known not to ask Gunn. Ragnar would have agreed with me."

"I don't know," Natalia said. "Raggers would think Ian's bet was hilarious. You know how much he loves cheating."

"Ugh, all these bloody pirates are stealing me money!" Valtra's black eyes flashed before honing in on Natalia. She jabbed an accusatory finger in Nat's direction. "And you."

Natalia put on her most ingenuous smile. "Yes?"

"You knew too."

"Knew what?"

"You knew about this whole," Valtra gesticulated as she searched for the word. "Scheme. Machination. Plot. Ian I get, since Sven needed him to change the access codes, but I'm the First bloody Mate of this boat. How in stardust did you learn about it before me?"

"Oh, well, I didn't exactly know," Natalia replied with false modesty. "But I had a good hypothesis." She took another bite of fruit for dramatic effect. "I was checking the message logs. The information is encrypted, of course, but by cross-referencing the ship's logs with fluctuations in energy signatures, you can make a pretty accurate guess about the message's destination. So I noticed Sven was corresponding with someone on Nifl."

Valtra's eyes narrowed. "Admiral Volsung."

Natalia nodded. "There's nothing of note on that backwater except for the former Admiral. So I figured, one way or another, Sven intended to make sure Alan would stay."

Valtra said nothing. She regarded Natalia with a hard, cryptic look. The silence extended uncomfortably long, but Natalia ignored the sensation of discomfort, finishing her snack with a satisfying crunch.

"Tasty," she said with a smile, swallowing the last bite.

Valta blinked before bursting into laughter. "Nat, you're as scummy as they come, you know that? A real bloody pirate queen in the making, eh?"

Natalia winked. "That's the plan."

Valtra let the mop lean against the wall before pulling Nat into a headlock and ruffling her hair. "Never trust a Jiordson not to cheat, eh?"

"I'm just here to make my family proud."

"All right, girl," Valtra said as she collected her mop and bucket. "I'm not even mad anymore. You won fair and square."

"By some definition?"

"That's as good as it gets on the Swallow, lass," Valtra confirmed. "A victory on a technicality is still a victory. And tonight we make Ian pay for everyone's drinks. Spirits know he's more than good enough for it."

Natalia let out a cheer. Drinking on someone else's dime was something she could get behind.

OPERATION 11:
THICKER THAN WATER

Alan rested his chin on his hand as he scrolled through the records he'd pulled up on the terminal. It had been several weeks since Ian dropped the name with the suggestion that Alan look into it, but in Alan's defense, it had been a busy past few weeks.

He was just now settling into his duties as Attaché Inspector of Observation — a frankly ridiculous title that Alan had yet to become accustomed to. His duties involved observing missions assigned to the Swallow while providing non-sensitive information about the Elite to Captain Jiordson in what amounted to an exchange program. That and paperwork. For a position the Chief Inspector had presumably concocted out of thin air as part of the hostage negotiations, she'd managed to include a lot of paperwork. He needed to write reports both for the Pyrean Navy and the Elite, and while Alan was more than up to the task, he could hear Colin laughing at him from halfway across the galaxy.

That's what you get for not escaping sooner, Colin would say, if he heard Alan's grumbling. And Colin was not entirely wrong.

But paperwork aside, the job was interesting enough. He got to sail on a pyrean naval vessel and join most, if not all, of the officer's meetings. Compared to his duties while investigating an open case, this was practically a vacation.

There had been little activity required of the Swallow since Alan's "promotion," so he was using part of his free time to skim declassified records within the Pyrean Navy.

The Crimson Raptor had been captained by General Hildegarde Jiordson. She died at forty, being was one of the youngest pyreans to reach the rank of general in the Navy. Despite her short career, her naval genius had been legendary. Now that Alan thought about it, he had a vague recollection of reading about her before — perhaps in one of his pyrean tactical history courses.

Hildegarde Jiordson, eldest child of Admiral Sebastian Jiordson. Admiral Jiordson was known to Alan through his reputation and actions in modern times. He was one of the most prominent figures in the Piracy Division of the Pyrean Navy, despite the Pyrean Navy having few public records about which ships served in that infamous division.

Alan looked over the records on the Crimson Raptor's destruction. It had been attacked by a guerrilla vessel while in pyrean territory and destroyed. Hildegarde and most of the crew had gone down with the ship. Only two people survived the Raptor's destruction — the then First Mate Ian Torrens, and Sven Jiordson, who was Hildegard's younger brother and at the time a registered civilian.

Sven was a child when he'd witnessed the tragedy. The Raptor had been between missions in what amounted to a routine trip for maintenance from one well-known safe harbor to another. Presumably the reason Sven had been allowed on board was because the journey was so routine and so safe. No doubt it was for those same reasons that the Raptor had been caught off-guard. What would have been a delightful field trip for a young lad in a career pirate family had turned into a grim loss both for the Pyrean Navy and the Jiordson family.

The report was brief — far shorter than Alan would have expected given such an unexpected loss of a Raptor-class vessel —

but it included a photo of the two survivors. Sven, a tiny scrap of a boy with his hallmark shock of lilac hair and luminous green eyes, was halfway hidden behind Ian Torrens. Ian was also recognizable, even if the man looked more clean-shaven then than he did now, but otherwise he had not aged much in the twenty-nine years since the incident.

Alan's eyes widened. Twenty nine years since the incident. Alan opened a new terminal and pulled up Sven's profile. As an official attaché, Alan had access to Elite records again, which included a short dossier on the Merry Swallow's captain. Sven Jiordson. Forty-one years old.

Fourteen years older than Alan.

Alan thumped his forehead on the desk before cradling his hands around his head to lessen his growing headache. Not only did pyreans age more slowly than humans, the developmental milestones were so different that there was no good way to compare ages between the two species. Alan knew this on an intellectual level, but it was hard not to think of Sven as a boy — a recent graduate from the Academy at best. Not someone who'd been traveling on star vessels longer than Alan had been alive.

With a sigh, Alan raised his head enough to close the reports. He wondered if he was supposed to ask Sven about the Raptor. Offering condolences this late into their relationship felt awkward, but the whole situation was awkward now that Alan knew.

Sven didn't seem to take anything seriously, but he rarely spoke about his older sister except in passing mentions of her reputation. Alan had assumed Sven's air of regret and sadness was a reflection of him failing to live up to her. It only now occurred to Alan that there might be a deeper sorrow — the sort of wound that even three decades of time and distance couldn't heal.

As Alan mulled over his options, the door opened with a soft swish. "Ow, ow, ow. Okay, Eric. That's naughty. No claws. Bad iguana! Bad!"

Eric was perched on Sven's head, looking as smug as a lizard could. With some effort, Sven at last managed to disentangle the reptile, and set him on his perch in the corner. Eric waggled his dewlap in victory as Sven wandered away, rubbing his scalp with a wince.

"Ugh," Sven said, throwing himself face-first onto his bed.

Alan folded his arms and leaned back in his seat. He gave Eric a mild look of condemnation. "Eric, don't bully Sven."

Eric smacked his mouth. Even after several weeks of living with the iguana, Alan couldn't tell how far the genetic modification went in terms of the animal's intelligence. That didn't stop Alan from trying to negotiate, though, and while Alan couldn't prove it, it seemed to be helping.

"It's not Eric," Sven groaned. With a dramatic flop, he managed to flip himself onto his back to stare up at the ceiling. "It's my dad."

Alan felt his ears perk. The inspector in him couldn't help feeling nosy, even if Sven was just venting — not divulging information on military strategy or pyrean politics.

"He's coming here. They're all coming here." Sven buried his face in his hands. "All the admirals with a position in the Piracy Division. On my ship. In a week."

Alan blinked. "What?"

"Yes, exactly. They're having an in-person conference to discuss concerns regarding the ma'jenn, and it turns out the Swallow is in an ideal sector of space to host them."

"Why not use their own vessels?" Alan wondered aloud. "The Swallow is tiny. Wouldn't one of the Raptor-classes be better for this sort of thing?"

Sven peeked through his fingers to regard Alan with a look of despair. "Take a guess, Attaché Inspector of Observation."

Between Sven's meaningful look and tone, Alan picked up on the hints.

"Ah," he said. "Me."

"Yes, you. The first human to become a sanctioned member on a Pyrean Navy vessel. And one in the Piracy Division no less."

Alan rested his cheek on his hand. "So what? They have their conference and get to stare at me like I'm some sort of zoo animal during their coffee breaks?"

"I already can't take it," Sven agreed.

"You're not the one on display here," Alan protested mildly, but Sven looked so unhappy, Alan didn't feel like fighting him on that point.

The door to their room flew open, and Natalia bound in without so much as a knock. Natalia had no respect for Sven's privacy or personal space — a fact Alan had become accustomed to in the relatively short amount of time he'd lived in Sven's quarters. On at least two occasions since Alan had become Attaché Inspector, Natalia had burst in early in the morning to chatter a long stream of words that ended in a cheerful extortion of money. Sven, clearly not a morning person, had done little more than flop around like a landed fish, before Nat espied his wallet and snatched up most of the money therein. Both times, she'd skipped out of the room with a pleasant "thank you and goodbye" before Sven managed a coherent reply.

This time had all the hallmarks of such a visit as Natalia careened onto the bed next to Sven, but rather than ask for money, she smashed him upside the head with his pillow. Her curly hair, pulled into a tight braid, bounced around in delight.

"Can you believe Dad is coming here?" She crowed. "And with all the other admirals? It's going to be a disaster, Sven. Nothing will be good enough for him."

Her tone was far too cheery and smug given the words she spoke.

Sven caught the pillow in between her smacks and gave her a dark look. "What? You think he's going to be so busy being disappointed in me that he spares clucking over you?"

She beamed. "That's the hope!"

"Well, bad news, Nat," Sven replied with grim amusement. "Mom is coming too."

Nat's grip on the pillow weakened, and her already pale face somehow blanched further. "Mom...?"

With as much dramatic flare as her brother, Natalia fell back to the bed as if wounded. "Mom is coming too? Why? To make sure I get the hint that I should've already graduated from the Academy by now?"

Alan gave the siblings the space to behave like clowns for a few moments longer before cutting in, "Come on, you two. Will it really be that bad?"

His thoughts were of his own parents. His relationship with his father had been rocky since the family had left Nibel for Earth. Once on the human homeworld, Sir Beringer insisted that his children should behave according to Earth customs, and Alan, a child then, had been more fearful for his mother's health than concerned about a new set of social mores. This had led to frequent heartache and misunderstandings, and while they'd managed a more equitable, intellectual discourse once Alan learned to navigate the politics of noble life on Earth, the damage had been done. Yet regardless of how much Alan clashed with his father regarding Alan's choices and behaviors, their mutual love and respect for the deceased Lady Beringer ensured these interactions remained civil.

Natalia's whole body slumped.

"No, probably not," she agreed at last. "But you'll understand when you meet them. They're...high achievers."

Admiral Jiordson was an active-duty officer in the Pyrean Navy, but Alan wasn't familiar with their mother. Natalia seemed to read his expression, so she explained, "Mom is a professor at the Academy. Naval Strategies and Tactics. She was a Vice Admiral before leaving active duty to teach full time."

"Oh." Alan looked surprised. "Er...my apologies. I didn't realize..."

He trailed off, realizing there was no polite way to say was he was thinking.

"You didn't realize how prestigious our family is?" Natalia said for him.

Alan coughed in embarrassment before turning away.

Sven sat up and crossed his legs. He wore a wistful expression that didn't suit his normally cheerful features. "Becoming a captain at thirty-seven is a lot less impressive when your big sis was a general by the same age, huh?"

Alan felt a chill run through him at the casual mention of Hildegarde Jiordson. Sven's words held no bitterness directed at her, containing only self-deprecation. As if Sven had somehow failed to live up to his sister's legacy by remaining a mere captain.

"Um, I, er, learned only recently about General Jiordson," Alan stammered, the guilt of prying finally getting the better of him. "I...I just wanted to offer you — "

Sven threw his pillow at Alan's face, cutting him off before he could finish. As the pillow tumbled to the ground, Alan glared at Sven with reproachful look. The boy flashed a soft smile to say how much he didn't want this conversation right now.

"Let's just figure out how to get you through this without it becoming a 'zoo' experience, 'kay, Alan?"

<hr>

THE DAY OF THE CONFERENCE, Sven joined the officer's morning meeting dressed in a formal pea coat and cravat. His mess of hair, usually barely restrained by a bandana, was pulled back into a tight ponytail as short as Alan's.

He looks like an actual captain, Alan mused.

All the officers had dressed for the occasion as well. Alan had never seen them in more formal clothes before with the exception of Gunnar, who wore a uniform during his shifts. It was a little surreal, and knowing their personalities, felt a bit like a costume party. Ragnar had traded his black tank top and fishnet gloves for a tight-fitting black coat, and while Valtra, who couldn't be bothered with a full uniform, wore a traditional loose tunic and fitted pants instead of her typical workout shirts and shorts. Ulrich was in his formal marine uniform as the Master at Arms, and Katja wore a slightly less rumpled medical jacket, her hair in a slightly more tidy bun.

Alan entertained a brief moment of wondering what Ian would look like in his uniform, but he wasn't entirely surprised when Ian breezed into the room wearing his usual coat and long gloves, a cigarette tucked behind an ear. If Alan squinted he could imagine his hair was more combed than usual, but it was a stretch.

Sven looked at Ian with open horror. "What are you wearing?!"

Ian gave him a flat look. "Clothes."

"Where is your uniform, Officer Torrens?" Sven said with increasing urgency, his hands balled into trembling fists.

"Sven, you need to calm down. I'll be in the engine room the whole time. These sorts of meetings aren't my style."

Sven bounced up to Ian. "Ian, you have to take this seriously. It's my dad and mom. They're both going to be on my ship. This is the first time they'll be on the Swallow since I was promoted to captain, and you're going to be standing around practically undressed?"

Ian was so tall and Sven so short that Sven had the air of a small dog yapping at a giant mastiff more than he looked like the captain of this vessel. Ian let out a long suffering sigh before patting Sven gently on his head.

"Sven, take a breath. Your dad's used to me. I've known him almost as long as you have. And I've been at these conferences more times than I care to count. This isn't a ship inspection. They'll go to their conference room, discuss the issues for a few days, and then when it finishes, they'll have some sort of soiree before everyone leaves. And I promise I'll dress up for that, okay?"

Still giving Ian a piteous look, Sven managed to nod before hopping up to snatch the cigarette behind Ian's ear. Without ceremony, he tossed it in the trash bin.

"But no smoking until it's over."

"Oh c'mon!" Ian muttered. "I'll go to the designated areas."

"Only once it's over," Sven insisted. He turned back to the other officers, who seemed content to let Ian face the brunt of Sven's anxiety on his own. "Right, and that goes for all of you. We make this as smooth as possible. Ulrich, make sure every admiral has an escort at all times while on the Swallow."

"Aye."

"Valt, you'll be in command while I'm attending this conference, but Professor Jiordson will probably want to spend some time with Natalia. If you have the time, can you make sure Nat is on her best behavior when she does?"

"Aye-aye, I was planning for it." Valtra gave a lazy salute, her expression suggesting she already knew she was in for babysitting duty.

"Gunnar and Ragnar, I need you ready to handle any requests the admirals have. I've given you dossiers on all attendant officers that are coming with them. I'd like you two to coordinate with those officers once they're on board."

"Aye-Aye, Captain," Gunnar said with a serious nod.

Ragnar just waved. "Gotcha, Capt."

"Katja," Sven said, turning to his Chief Medical Officer. "I sure hope we don't need you, but be ready for anything."

"Always am, Capt."

"And finally, Alan." Sven met Alan's eyes for the first time since the officer's meeting started. "You're with me in a formal capacity as an Elite attaché."

Alan looked skeptical. "You really think the admirals will let me join in their meetings?"

"Any meeting I'm allowed in, you'll be joining," Sven insisted. "But I anticipate at least a few of the meetings will be closed even to me. That said, I think you're going to have some interesting insights into the situation given your background."

Alan nodded. Sven was correct that Alan was an ideal fit as an advisor, but the whole situation remained boggling and uncomfortable.

Before Alan had become Attaché Inspector of Observation and been given a higher level of clearance on the Merry Swallow, he'd believed, like other Elite inspectors, that the Pyrean Navy's Piracy Division was a branch of the Navy created to commit acts of piracy. He'd been taught that the supposed mission of the branch — the eradication and prevention of piracy — was an excuse to keep the branch's existence, unofficial or no, from violating human-pyrean treaties.

Yet every document Alan could find from the Pyrean Navy's side confirmed that the Piracy Division was in fact an anti-piracy branch. This branch just happened to self-fund through small-scale, controlled acts of piracy. Tolls, they called them in the literature. Funding safer star travel for all.

The IPC's willingness to host Alan made so much more sense in this context, since the ship's job description was almost exactly the same as the task forces that worked under Alan when he'd been a more orthodox inspector of the Elite.

By all accounts, the Piracy Division could use someone like Alan. The assault on the Popinjay was not an isolated incident. Multiple attacks had occurred over the past Universal year, and while casualties were low — nothing at all like the attack on the Crimson Raptor three decades earlier — it suggested something more than just the unrelated, uncoordinated attacks of common brigands.

The IPC could discount human involvement given the level of technology used in the attacks, but there was debate within the Piracy Division whether the ma'jenn's Moon Empire was directly involved, or if these acts of piracy came from some faction outside the control of both the IPC and the Empire. The four Piracy Division admirals were here to discuss all of these possibilities before the Navy had an official meeting with representatives from the Empire, which was scheduled for the near horizon.

Despite the unusual circumstances in which Alan had found himself, he could feel his investigator's curiosity tingling. The pyreans and ma'jenn had been trade partners for millennia, but even pyrean records on the Moon Empire were limited. Human contact with ma'jenn was almost non-existent. Alan had encountered half a dozen ma'jenn in person during his entire childhood on Nibel plus his time working for the Elite.

He could only imagine how jealous Colin would be when the report came in, and that thought alone was enough to make Alan smile in satisfaction.

ADMIRAL JIORDSON WAS the last of the admirals to board. Sven stood with his back straight, cheerful features pulled into an unusually grave expression of formality beside Alan, as he greeted each admiral one by one and granted them official permission to come aboard. His manners were impeccable.

Valtra stood beside Sven at attention as well, but she said nothing — her presence was a formality, while Ulrich, Ragnar, and Gunnar greeted the attendant officers as part of their duties for this conference. None of them acknowledged Alan, which Alan didn't mind. He was used to playing host at equivalent events within the Elite, so being a background figure was a pleasant change.

Once the other admirals had been officially welcomed, it was Admiral Jiordson's turn to stand before Sven. Alan kept his face forward, but he couldn't help assessing the man out the corner of his eye. Looking at Sebastian Jiordson and Sven Jiordson side by side, it was clear they were father and son. Yet despite some shared familial thread in the overall features, the details were different. Sebastian was broad-shouldered and tall — only slightly shorter than Ian. His hair was purple, but unlike Sven's gradated lavender, the admiral's hair was dark and heavily shot with gray. Once he might have looked as boyish as Sven, but his features had become rugged and severe with age, accented by a neat goatee and an eyepatch. The missing eye was a souvenir from his youth as a pirate captain, but he'd elected not to take a prosthetic replacement for reasons the reports didn't make clear.

He stood with Idel Jiordson. While both of their children had inherited Sebastian's clear green eyes and pale skin, Natalia's hair and facial features were a reflection of their mother. Like her daughter, Idel had thick, tight waves of blonde hair, which she kept in rows of small, intricate braids looped across her scalp. They were pulled up into an elegant knot before spilling in curls down her back. Her skin and eyes were honey brown, and unlike the rest of the guests, she wore civilian clothes — a dress of pale blue silks accented with silver and carrying a fan to match.

Professor Jiordson was smiling. Her husband was not.

"Admiral Jiordson, Professor Jiordson. Welcome to the Merry Swallow. Please make yourselves at home during your visit."

"Captain Jiordson," Sebastian said in an equally formal tone. "We accept your invitation. Thank you for hosting this conference on such short notice."

"Oh, it's good to see you, Sven," Idel said, pulling him into a hug. "You really should visit more."

"Mom, not now," Sven hissed in a low voice that only Alan and Idel could hear.

"I left the Navy for a reason, Sven," Idel murmured, only marginally loosening her grip. "I get to do things like this now."

"I know, but —"

Idel released Sven, but she continued to look him over. Although she seemed to be fretting about his appearance, clucking under her breath about how well he'd been eating, Alan could see her gaze shifting to observe Alan. She assessed Alan with a sharp look even as she continued to mother her son.

Sebastian coughed, but Idel ignored him. The other admirals must have realized it was better to ignore this family reunion rather than intervene, and they began to walk down the hallway to the meeting room with Ulrich and his team.

"Where's Natalia, Sven?" Idel asked after a moment. "Isn't she going to come see us?"

"Er...here, Mom," Natalia turned the corner. "Sorry I'm late."

Natalia had put up her hair as well, pulled into a series of braids, which were not quite as precise or neat as her mother's. She wore an embroidered tunic with baggy pants and a silk wrap, but unlike her mother, she looked uncomfortable in the elegant civilian garb.

"Oh Natalia," Idel rushed to hug her and even Sebastian moved to join his wife, smiling softly in a way he hadn't for Sven. "We miss you so much. I hear this year's crop of first-years are delightful. I think you really would love the Academy if you just gave it a try, my dear."

"I like it here, Mom," Natalia said weakly.

"They're doing right by you, my lass?" Sebastian said in such an openly worried, sweet tone, Alan's eyebrows shot up in surprise. He looked to Sven, who just shook his head. Any explanation would have to wait till later. "Sven is taking care of you? Keeping you safe?"

"I don't need him to take care of me, Dad!" Natalia said with a nervous laugh.

As Alan watched the two prestigious guests continue to fuss over their daughter without any consideration for decorum, he remembered the photo of Hildegarde, pulled up during his search into the Crimson Raptor. Now that Alan thought about it, Natalia was an almost perfect image of Hildegarde. Younger, but similar in features, born close to a decade after her sister's death.

The golden child returned to the family.

Natalia had mentioned once that her father was a little over-protective, but Alan hadn't understood the connotations at the time. Now the pieces fell into place. Alan glanced at Sven out the corner of his eye, but the man remained stiff and expressionless, eyes fixed on his father, their green depths for once inscrutable.

Everyone has their family troubles, Alan supposed.

Operation 12: A New Strategy

ALAN REALIZED his presence at the conference was a mistake before the proceedings began. As soon as he entered with Sven, all four admirals, as well as their attendant officers, gave him venomous looks. Only Idel did not look actively hostile, but her pleasant smile was unreadable as she watched him follow her son into the meeting.

The message was clear. His presence on the ship would be tolerated, but he was not welcome. Sven had hinted that it was Tristan von Volsung himself who'd pushed for Alan's current position on Swallow, and Tristan had been an Admiral close to fifty years earlier. From the dossiers on these current admirals, at least three of the four had overlapped as an admiral during Tristan's time in the Piracy Branch.

Tristan was remembered as the Pirate King of the Fifth Octant more than he was as Admiral Volsung. It was a fanciful title evoking a romantic age of freedom and exploration — notions which the pyreans treasured. Yet running a fleet was not about wanderlust or whims or derring-do. It was about organization, precision, and communication. It occurred to Alan that Tristan's status as a folk hero among pyrean privateers might not be how his peers in the service remembered him.

"Jiordson," Alan murmured for Sven's ears only. "It might be best if —"

Sven didn't acknowledge Alan's words, but his face hardened. Rather than address Alan to cut off Alan's protests, he announced to the rest of the room, "Admirals, at this time I'd like to introduce you to Elite Attaché Inspector of Observation Alan Beringer. He has recently joined our crew and will be assisting me during this conference."

Alan forced his face into a smooth mask as he adjusted his train of thought. Executing a precise bow with a calculated amount of respect — neither flippant nor obsequious — he said in United Pyrean, "It is my pleasure, Admirals."

"The rat can speak," an attendant officer muttered from the back in Fimmelian. Alan wasn't an expert in that particular pyrean language, but he knew enough to get the gist.

Alan bit his lip, holding back an equally snide retort. He'd worked enough cases with enough difficult local authorities that dealing with attitude was nothing unusual or unexpected. And regardless of any personal insults Alan received, Sven had enough stress related to this conference — he didn't need Alan adding to it.

Thus Alan wasn't expecting Sven to all but snarl, "Inspector Beringer is here as my aide." The sheer force behind the words startled Alan. He looked over in surprise at Sven, who was fuming, all but shaking, as he continued, "I will happily leave this discussion if you wish it, Admirals, but you will treat my assistant with the same respect you treat me."

The officer looked down, while Admiral Jiordson raised a mollifying hand. "There is no need for incivility, officers. We are here to discuss the situation with the ma'jenn, and while having an Elite inspector as an aide is...unorthodox, we respect your decision, Captain Jiordson."

These words diffused some of the tension in the room, and Alan released the breath he hadn't realized he'd been holding. For the next couple hours, the meeting continued without incident but without any progress either.

There was little discussion beyond what Alan already gleaned from the reports Sven had provided him. The Moon Empire had requested a meeting with the Pyrean Navy, which would take place two Universal weeks from now. It was unclear what the meeting entailed, but the admirals were convinced it would be a power play seeking greater concessions within the current pyrean-ma'jenn treaties. The empress had announced she would be stepping down as supreme leader to work in an advising role now that her successor had come of age. Ma'jenn thought of time differently from both humans and pyreans, so whether this change in power would happen in the next year or the next three decades, it was hard to guess. Regardless, this meant a turning point in the dynasty. Such transitions of power happened infrequently given the life span of the ma'jenn, and as the meeting progressed it became clear to Alan that this political situation was of more concern than the unsanctioned attacks themselves.

"They'll be dragging up grievances from the first dynasty," one of the admirals was saying. She drummed her fingers on the table with irritation. "Those mutts live so long as it is, we don't even have clear records on protocols during these times."

"Nor do we have any ambassadors in the Court itself," another added.

Only half-listening, Alan found himself scrolling through the reports he'd collated for this meeting. Politics is what leadership does in both species, he realized. Just as the Chief Inspector spent more time talking to the HIA and managing relations with its other departments than working cases, so would admirals worry more about interspecies relations than conducting an investigation.

This investigation was ongoing, Alan learned, but it remained inconclusive. Thus, with their meeting approaching, the admirals now worked under the assumption that the ma'jenn had developed jamming technology to support tactical space strikes and were planning to enter a more aggressive period under the new successor.

It was a neat theory that, on the surface, tied together this transition of power with escalating hostilities by the ma'jenn, but as an Elite Inspector, Alan found everything about it unsatisfying. From what little Alan knew, and what all pyrean records showed, the ma'jenn were not and had never been a warlike people. While they had a weapons development program, it was on a much smaller scale than their research into terraforming and civil engineering. In fact, many of their so-called weapons technology were modified terraforming techniques. While these recent jumps in technology could be secret projects that pyrean intel had failed to uncover, it seemed unlikely. Similarly, the fact that the Moon Empire would choose to target relatively small vessels in undisputed sectors of space with its supposed secret weapon didn't make political sense.

Yet these admirals insisted the Navy had no knowledge of the sensor jammers they'd encountered during these recent attacks, which meant it must be an outside agent rather than a rogue Navy vessel. If both Alan and the admirals were correct, ruling out both pyreans and ma'jenn, that meant the attackers were either humans or some hitherto undiscovered starfaring species. He doubted either theory would feel compelling, especially coming from a human, so he kept his mouth shut as the debate went in circles.

This whole conference was going to be a waste of time, he realized, and this was only the first half of the first day's session. Two additional Pyrean Standard days has been reserved for these meetings. It became clear why Ian was hiding in engineering, and Valtra was more than willing to helm the ship in Sven's absence. As Alan tried to find a reasonable excuse to get him out of attending (but maybe not entirely abandoning Sven), he noticed Sven's face growing darker and more frustrated by the second.

It was as if Sven was thinking everything Alan was, but unlike Alan, he seemed to have run out of patience.

"Admirals," Sven said, standing up from his seat before Alan could try to talk him down. "While I realize this upcoming meeting with ma'jenn emissaries is of the utmost importance, we are ignoring the concerns related to these recent acts of aggression against naval vessels in pyrean-controlled space. While I do not discount that the ma'jenn may be behind it, Inspector Beringer has been looking into — "

"I'm not sure why you think a human's opinion on this is at all relevant to our discussion, Captain," one of the admirals cut in.

Alan tried not to wince. He'd expected this exact reaction, and Sven should have known enough to cut his losses. Yet from the look in Sven's eyes, it was clear the captain had no intention of backing down despite the warning in his superior's tone.

"I think his opinion might be relevant given he is a member of the Elite," Sven countered. "If we're here to investigate unsanctioned acts of piracy, surely using an Elite inspector as a resource is worth our while."

"Our own investigation will provide all the information we need," the admiral countered.

"With all due respect, I'm not sure," Sven continued.

Alan folded his hands in front of his face to hide his mouth as he muttered, "Drop it, Jiordson."

But it seemed Sven would not drop it. Sven's eyes flickered to Alan for only a moment before he turned back to the admiral.

"The Swallow was the first ship to respond to the Popinjay's distress signal. That assault looked nothing like any encounter I've had with the ma'jenn. I stated as much then, and I will restate that now. Inspector Beringer has begun looking into the patterns across all attacks by unidentified vessels over the past year, and —"

"That's enough, Captain," another admiral interrupted. "We have read your report, and at this time, we have more important matters to discuss." When Sven opened his mouth to protest, the admiral rose from her seat. "Enough, I said. I am aware of how you used your connections to Tristan von Volsung to get his descendant a place on this ship, and I am not impressed or amused by your actions. Volsung's marriage to that human was a disgrace to us all, and you think what? That if you show off your pet we'll be impressed? Treat him as though he is a pyrean?"

"That Volsung," another admiral muttered with a shake of his head. "I swear he married that wench just to mock us."

Alan closed his eyes and ground his teeth to hold back his temper. Whatever Alan thought about his great grandfather, he thought less of his great grandfather's former colleagues. It was one thing to accomplish nothing as they talked in circles, but now they'd decided to hurl mud at his family members. If this was what Tristan had put up with during his time in the admiralty, it was no wonder he retired early.

"With all due respect, Sir," Sven said in a trembling voice, "You have no right to —"

"Enough." It was Admiral Jiordson who cut in this time. "Enough, Captain. We thank you for your hospitality aboard your ship, but these proceedings shall continue behind closed doors. If you will excuse us?"

The way Sven glared at his father, Alan felt a flare of concern that he might disobey the implied command, but with all eyes on him and Sven, there was no way Alan could try to talk Sven down in the moment. Fortunately Sven managed to regain some of his composure.

"Understood, Admiral," Sven said at last, executing a crisp salute. He turned on his heel and left the room. Alan bowed with a graciousness he did not feel before following.

Sven did not speak or acknowledge Alan as they walked. Alan followed, but he was unsure where Sven intended to go. Surely not to the bridge, which was practically adjacent to the meeting room, nor to his room or the gardens, it seemed, as he passed by both the living quarters and the lift to the upper decks. Sven made his way to a quieter part of the ship use for maintenance. When it had been several corridors since they passed another crew member, Sven cut into a narrow side corridor, out of sight of the main hallway before slamming his fist against the wall.

"Those arrogant, complacent fools," Sven snarled. Never had Alan seen him so furious. "As if they know the first thing about sailing or surprise attacks. Easy not to care about ambushes when you have a whole fleet escorting you. Why not just pick the easiest answer and ignore the facts?" Sven all but shook with anger. "The Popinjay was lucky. Other ships that went down lost sailors in the ambushes, but what? Ma'jenn politics are more important than our lives?"

Alan folded his arms. "I'm sure they believe they are correct, Sven. When you control the starways and have the biggest guns in the galaxy, it's easy to imagine you also have all the facts."

"And my father." Sven leaned his forehead against the metal paneling. "He dismisses me on my own ship? Allows those pompous asses to insult you and the Volsung family lineage in the same breath?" His hand curled into a fist before he slammed it again into the wall. Once, then twice, but before the third time, Alan grabbed it, holding the fist so Sven couldn't hurt himself further.

Sven tried to yank his arm free from Alan's grip, but when Alan didn't budge, he looked up with a wild, pitiful expression. Alan had never seen Sven on the verge of tears before, but he recognized the signs.

"It wouldn't be like this if Hilde were here," Sven whispered. "She'd be an admiral by now. She'd...she'd..."

The look in Sven's eyes broke Alan's heart. Memories of Alan's mother rose to the forefront of his thoughts. How many times had Alan imagined her alive in some time or place long after her passing? The words she would have said, the comfort she'd have brought him? The knowledge that a small piece of the universe would forever be missing? Before Alan could stop himself, he pulled Sven into a tight, fierce hug.

"I'm sorry," he whispered, knowing how inadequate those words were yet having nothing else to offer.

Despite everything, Sven seemed to understand the gesture. He wrapped his arms around Alan and buried his face in Alan's chest. "I should be the one apologizing," he muttered. "I didn't think...I didn't think they'd treat you like this."

"I know it's not much comfort, but this is about what I expect when my mixed heritage is involved," Alan murmured with a humorless smile. "My feelings about Tristan aren't the only reason I prefer to pass as a full human. I went through the same thing with my superiors when joining the Elite. Though for the opposite reasons, as you can imagine." After a moment, he added, "That said, Tristan knows how to make enemies, doesn't he?"

Sven laughed but it sounded a little like a sob. He hugged Alan tighter. "Hilde got to know him while she was growing up. Once she graduated from the Academy, they became good friends. She was the one who told me all the stories about him. My dad had a rockier relationship with him, especially after Tristan retired, but I assumed he thought of Tristan as his comrade, if not a close friend. At least I thought they respected each other."

Sven looked down as if in disappointment — as if coming to a realization he didn't want to have.

"Regardless of what your father may think," Alan replied in a gentle tone, "Admiral Jiordson is here in a room with three of his current colleagues while Tristan is living a hermit's life somewhere on Nilf. I am sure Admiral Jiordson is weighing the politics of the situation over personal feelings."

Alan stepped back enough to put his hands on Sven's shoulders and give him a little shake. "Which you could stand to do a bit more of in these situations, Captain."

Sven dropped his head. "You're right. I know. But I couldn't stand it. That conversation was driving me to madness."

Alan laughed. "Don't misunderstand, Sven. I agree with everything you said and feel, but sometimes you have to accept a lost cause when you see it."

Sven managed a weak smile. He'd seemed to have regained

some of his composure, which made Alan heave a sigh of relief. Absently he brushed at a stray strand of Sven's hair, which had escaped the tight ponytail.

"Being dismissed was the best outcome," Alan insisted, tucking the stand behind Sven's ear. "I don't think either of us would survive another two days of that. Our time is better spent conducting an actual investigation rather than sitting in that room feeling sorry for ourselves."

"I agree, Inspector," Idel said from behind Alan.

Alan startled. He realized his hand was still hovering by Sven's face, and he pulled it back as if burned.

"P-professor Jiordson, why are you —"

"Here?" she cut in. "Partly I wanted to check on my son, though it seems he is in good hands." Her tone was innocuous, but Alan felt himself blush as though her words were insinuating something. "But also I've come to the same conclusion you have and decided my time was better spent on the other side of those closed doors."

She snapped her fan open with a decisive clack before fanning herself, her face half hidden. "I'd forgotten what those meetings with admirals were like, if I'm being completely honest. I'm used to dealing with at most one or two at a time. Four is far too many."

"And Dad agrees with you?" Sven asked, searching her face as he spoke.

"That's a complicated question, Sven," Idel admitted. "Probably, given that he asked me, an outside expert, to join him here. But as a whole, the Navy is more concerned with the ma'jenn succession of power. They want to maintain a strong, unified front if the new empero decides to renegotiate the treaties. And I suspect there's a chance that if this supposed investigation digs too deeply, they may not find answers they like."

Alan's eyes narrowed. "So you suspect pyreans?"

Idel snapped her fan shut and gave Alan a bright smile. "Shall we adjourn to a more private place to continue this discussion?"

THE MERRY SWALLOW wasn't a large ship, so the most private place ended up being Sven's quarters. Alan felt a part of himself die as Idel looked around the utilitarian bedroom, took note of Alan's bed and belongings on his side of the room, then nodded to herself as if all the pieces had fallen into place.

It's not like that, Alan wanted to say, but he knew as a professional investigator that when it came to the possibility of self-incrimination, it was best to say nothing at all.

Alan cleared his throat, while Sven pulled off his coat and cravat and tossed them on the bed. Idel took a seat by the table, her beautiful silk dress looking out of place amid the plain furniture.

"Please, Professor Jiordson," Alan said, "I'd like to hear more of your theories."

"I'm hardly an investigator like yourself, Inspector Beringer," Idel began as a disclaimer. She leaned back in her seat as she studied the end of her fan. "But I am quite familiar with naval tactics. Without getting into the details, while the overall nature of stellar naval tactics may have not changed much in the last few millennia, many of the details change quite radically as suits the available technology. You can tell a lot about tactics if you know something about the level of technology, and vice versa."

She set her fan on the table and crossed her legs. "Seb asked me to look over the reports on these strike before coming, but if I'm honest, it's more confusing than clarifying. Technology aside, the tactics themselves match the textbook maneuvers of thirty years ago. Completely uninspired. If someone asked me to create tactics for ships with this hitherto unknown jamming technology that has left the Navy feeling outgunned and outmaneuvered, I would come up with something a bit more creative than isolated and relatively low-stakes hit-and-runs."

"So you're saying the tactics they're using haven't caught up with their ship technology?" Sven asked.

Idel smiled. "That is no doubt the conclusion the admirals in the other room have come to, but in my opinion, there aren't enough details in the reports to make such an assumption. About their ship's technology, I mean."

When Alan and Sven waited for her to continue the explanation, Idel elaborated, "The admirals insist the jamming techniques are nothing like anything we've seen and therefore must represent a major advancement. But advancement implies improvements in something like the material science or manufacturing techniques of the ships. This is certainly a possibility, but I'll let the engineers weigh in on that. I can only offer a perspective as a tactical officer, and you don't need technological advancements to win encounters. Focusing on the mystery of these jamming techniques distracts from the other facts in this case."

Alan tilted his head as he started to follow her line of thinking. "You believe they're bluffing?"

Idel's eyes lit up, as if delighted by Alan's conclusion. "Very good, Inspector Beringer," she said in the tone of a professor praising one of her students. "That is exactly what I believe."

"Bluffing alone won't take down a Jay-class vessel," Sven muttered in a dark tone.

"No," Idel agreed. "But the strikes are short, and they happen in unpopulated territories when the ships are least prepared. That suggests careful tactics and maybe some leaked intel — not an overwhelming difference in technologies. Why are the strike tactics so old-fashioned? Because the ships are in fact of an older — not newer — design, I'd argue. They're not suited to the current styles of modern engagement."

"But the jamming technology," Sven said in an insistent tone.

"It's unsettling," Idel agreed. "On the surface, it seems very powerful and dangerous, as if some outside force is invading our territory with an overwhelming technical advantage."

"But," Alan said as he reached Idel's logical conclusion, "Another possibility is that this opponent is already familiar with the Navy's sensors and response systems. They're using this knowledge to coordinate their strikes and obfuscate their actual advantage, which is that the Navy has some form of intel leak."

"I believe this is the case," Idel said. "But until Navy scientists figure out how these ships work, it's just a theory with no more substantiation than any other. And Seb says there's no evidence of a leak, which is why the other admirals feel comfortable dismissing it to focus their investigations on the ma'jenn."

Sven folded his arms as he considered this possibility. Alan had discussed some of these points with Sven earlier, but Idel had taken Alan's theories to an extreme that Alan had not been ready to consider. A leak in Pyrean Naval Intelligence was indeed a bold working assumption.

Yet Sven at last nodded as if it made as much sense as anything. "So they're targeting vessels in remote areas, not just because these ships make easier targets, but because those sorts of strikes leave less evidence for the Navy to analyze."

Idel's smile turned a little grim. "It makes at least as much sense as blaming the ma'jenn. If the ma'jenn wanted to send a message, they would do something more impactful than some shocking but largely ineffective skirmishes. Why would the Empire choose to show their hand via these one-off strikes?"

"So not the ma'jenn," Alan said.

"No, not the ma'jenn," Idel agreed. "I have no doubt about that. The ma'jenn have never shown any inclination to pre-emptive military strikes in our millennia of shared history, and this violates everything we know about their ships and methods of engagement."

"So you believe some pyrean faction has gained access to naval technology and intel and is using it against them?" Alan asked without trying to soften his words. There was no politic way to phrase it.

Idel snapped open her fan to stare along the gleaming edge. "The tactics are textbook pyrean. Why shouldn't we assume they're pyrean?" She gave Alan a considering look. "Don't mistake me for those admirals in the other room, Inspector

Beringer. I'm not here to find the most convenient narrative to suit my stellar view."

"Professor Jiordson, to me this then suggests a single opponent rather than numerous, unconnected incidents," Alan said.

"I agree," Idel replied with a nod. "Is it the same ship? Doubtful. Are the ships in some way affiliated? I'd wager a year's income on it. The ships and tactics share too many similarities to be unaffiliated bands that happen to have the same weapons dealer."

"This suggests a pirate confederacy of former Pyrean Navy crew members," Alan said, again cutting to the chase. He couldn't have been so straightforward with the admirals, but Idel Jiordson seemed like she could handle it.

"Yes, almost certainly," she agreed with a smile, as though Alan's bluntness entertained her. "The Navy tries to keep such organizations from growing too large, but it's not unprecedented. Ones of this size and scale of operation have happened on several occasions throughout history. Even the admirals would agree on this, if not for the ships themselves. Most unsanctioned pirates have outdated Navy vessels or modified merchant ships. Since these vessels use some unknown forms of technology, the admirals have convinced themselves of ma'jenn involvement despite more evidence to the contrary."

Alan leaned back and steepled his fingers. "So if we can explain where these ships came from, the admirals will have an easier time accepting pyrean involvement?"

Idel looked at Alan with open amusement. "I've never met an admiral who had an easy time swallowing being wrong, but yes, it will probably make it 'easier.' By some definition."

"Well," Alan replied with his own grim smile. "As much as I was hoping I'm wrong, there's an extremely straightforward answer to that mystery as well."

Operation 13: The Ma'jenn

The conference concluded as Alan expected. Three days of talks and little to nothing had been resolved before the admirals returned to their ships and dispersed. Sebastian Jiordson was the last admiral who remained on board, since Sven had requested a meeting with him before his departure. Idel waited in the officer's meeting room with Alan and Sven to ensure the admiral wouldn't leave prematurely. Alan and Idel lounged in chairs while Sven paced the room.

"He's not coming," Sven muttered.

"Hush, dear. Your father will come."

"He won't," Sven said flatly. "He's never listened to me before, why should he start now?"

"If you're so convinced, care to make a wager?"

Sven gave his mother a sour look before declining. Alan made a note not to take up any of the Jiordson clan on their wagers.

As if to prove Idel's point, the meeting room door opened and Sebastian strode in.

"Sven, I know this conference didn't go as you'd hoped, but —"

Sebastian stopped mid-sentence when he realized both Idel

and Alan were present as well. He eyed Alan before regarding his wife with open suspicion.

"What sort of ambush is this, Idel?"

"Ambush? My word. How frightful." Idel had switched out of her elegant formal gowns into a loose frilly blouse and tight pants with knee-high fitted boots as if she were off for a horse ride after this.

The fan remained, and Idel flared it open in mock surprise. "But speaking of ambushes...""

Sebastian's eye narrowed before he turned back to Sven. "Sven, you have every right to be angry with me, but —"

"Alan solved your case, Dad." Now that the other admirals weren't present, Sven had no hesitation interrupting his father. "And, no, it's not the ma'jenn."

Sebastian started when Sven cut him off, but he soon recovered enough to glare in Alan's direction. Alan met his gaze but said nothing, and at last Sebastian turned back to Sven.

"What? You expect me to believe some human figured out in three days what our intelligence teams couldn't determine in two months?"

Sven shrugged. "It was closer to five minutes with Mom's help, but he insisted on being thorough." Sven met Alan's eyes. Despite Sven's serious expression, Alan could have sworn Sven was on the verge of laughter. "It is one of his better, if more frustrating, qualities. I'd hoped to have this information before the conference ended, but one of his information channels only came through an hour earlier."

Sebastian looked between the three of them with the harried expression of a hunted man. He gave in with a sigh. "All right, just say it then. No need for this drama. What's your theory, Inspector Beringer?"

"I'll share my full report with you later, Admiral Jiordson, but to get to the point, the mysterious technology your team mistook for ma'jenn was —"

"Captain Jiordson," Gunnar's voice cut in on the overhead comms. "Please come to the bridge immediately. We have ma'jenn vessels Gating in. Their flagship is hailing us."

All three Jiordsons stood at once and headed toward the bridge. Alan, his mouth still hanging open for the big reveal, quietly shut it and trailed after them. He considered sharing his findings as they walked, but he could tell the admiral's mind was focused on the immediate situation, and he might not be receptive to Alan's conclusions right now.

The meeting room was located next to the bridge — no more than a couple paces — but by the time they arrived, the ma'jenn leader was waiting, projected on the bridge's viewscreen. This ma'jenn was petite and dusky-skinned with long white hair and deep violet bangs. Despite limited human-ma'jenn contact, Alan knew enough about ma'jenn culture to recognize the black robes and white shawl of a high-ranking priest. Priests did not sail on any random vessel. A priest's presence here suggested this was no accidental encounter.

Ragnar's words confirmed his suspicions. "There are close to a dozen smaller vessels in addition to the flagship. Even with Admiral Jiordson's escort, we're outnumbered. Their weapons are in standby, but they have us surrounded."

Sven nodded. "Take us off mute."

He looked at the ma'jenn priest and said in Interplanetary Standard, "This is Captain Jiordson of the Merry Swallow. To whom do I have the pleasure of speaking?"

The ma'jenn acknowledged Sven with a formal nod. "I am Corandisham y'Llaunau d'Helva. I serve as a high priest in the Crescent Court of Empress Elantira y'Xian d'Correno, may Her Light ever shine on the Empire."

A low murmur went through the Swallow's bridge crew. It seemed they were as startled as Alan. Members of the Court rarely left ma'jenn territories.

While pyreans knew little about the internal social structures of the ma'jenn, and humans knew even less, it was well-known that the ma'jenn were eusocial — a quality humans associated more with ants and bees than highly sentient lifeforms which had colonized the galaxy long before humans escaped Earth's gravity well. Like the ant and honey bee colonies of Earth, each ma'jenn hive had its own social hierarchy, but all individuals answered to the empero, which was the highest seat of power in the Moon Empire. Unlike the case in many Earth-based eusocial species, individual ma'jenn could reproduce, but they did so rarely — hardly surprising given how old ma'jenn could get. Reaching a millennium was not out of the question, and the current empress had been in power for close to six hundred years.

Beyond this, the ma'jenn had several noteworthy qualities. The first was their uncomfortably utopian society. They'd colonized numerous solar systems before the pyreans made contact with them, and beyond their advanced terraforming technologies, which made planetary resources almost unlimited, they had cheap and plentiful sources of energy. They followed some sort of caste system, as many other eusocial species did, but from the records of pyrean observers, this caste system was not rigid, nor was it clear how roles were assigned. Most ma'jenn preferred to avoid the other races outside of trade situations, but the few who decided to leave were allowed to do so, often choosing to live on mixed ma'jenn-pyrean world colonies, or forming small hives of their own beyond the authority of the Moon Empire.

The next notable quality was that ma'jenn didn't recognize gender outside of the supreme leader. The empero could choose the title of Emperor, Empress, or Empero, and of the historical records available in pyrean archives, several emperos of previous dynasties had chosen to remain agender. While the current empress chose her title over half a millennium earlier, any details about her successor, or their preferences, were unknown outside of the Crescent Court itself.

The final noteworthy quality of the ma'jenn was how cute they were. As a direct advisor to Empress Elantira, Corandisham was one of the most powerful people in the galaxy, but all Alan could think as he stared at them was that Corandisham was adorable. Alan didn't consider himself sentimental, but it was as his Elite training had warned. To his mammalian eyes, the short fur that covered the ma'jenn appeared velvety and soft, and with the ma'jenn's long, silky tufted ears and short, fluffy tails, they resembled Earth canids — and invoked that same heart-warming response.

Unlike canids, the ma'jenn had horns, which grew in a number of styles of varying length, number, and geometry (features of different ethnic groups, pyrean ethnographers conjectured), and Corandisham was no exception. A short gray horn protruded from the center of their forehead like a unicorn. A longer horn might have looked regal, but the tiny nub made the high priest of the Crescent Moon Court look even smaller and cuter.

Alan forced himself not to stare. He was fortunate that he wasn't the sort of person to needlessly smile — a facial expression that ma'jenn interpreted as an act of open hostility. Their ears and tails were the primary vehicles for displaying emotion, and smiling was equivalent to baring fangs.

"To what do I owe the pleasure of this meeting, High Priest Corandisham?" Sven kept his voice polite and his facial expression even.

Sven's composure took Alan by surprise even though he knew how important decorum was to the ma'jenn. On some level, Alan knew Sven was capable of it, but his formal language and posture made him look like an entirely different captain.

"It depends, Captain Jiordson," Corandisham replied. "We are anticipating a summit with representatives of the Pyrean Navy to discuss the growing piracy problem. Yet when we learned about this meeting between Navy admirals in such a remote a location, we could not help but investigate, given how close it is the appointed meeting time between our peoples. While I would prefer to show you proper respect with pleasantries, I will not insult your intelligence by taking any more time to get to the point. I will ask you directly, Captain Jiordson, is this timing a coincidence?"

Admiral Jiordson stepped forward to catch the viewscreen camera's focus. "High Priest Corandisham, I am Admiral Jiordson. As you are no doubt aware, I will be one of the Navy representatives in that upcoming meeting." The admiral gave the most minimal of bows. "At that time, I will be happy to address all of your concerns, but as you have been honest with us, so I will be honest with you. I take umbrage with your question and your methods. If you wished to enter space occupied by official Naval vessels, you should give proper notification. The Pyrean Navy has not violated any treaty or acted in any way deserving of such mistrust."

Corandisham crossed their legs, and their face expressed such supercilious distaste that the condescension was almost palpable.

"You would do well to remember, Admiral, that while the ma'jenn accept the pyrean's role as peace-keeper of the starways, we do so only because we have no interest in fighting or conflict. We agree to pyrean tolls because they are a fair exchange, even if your methods have always seemed...unusual. But this does not mean we are helpless, or that we will roll over if we decide the pyreans have stepped out of line."

Admiral Jiordson's single eye narrowed. After a considering moment of silence, he folded his arms. "What exactly are you implying, High Priest Corandisham?"

Corandisham leaned forward to glare through the viewscreen. "I am asking why the Navy has seen fit to hold a secret meeting, in the depths of space rather than on Pyre, right before your meeting with us? I am asking why, just as we announce the transition of power from one empero to the next, we see an increase in aggressive activity toward our vessels? More raids, more casualties. And yet you expect us to sit back meekly and wait for your excuses?" Corandisham rose from their seat. "Is this how the IPC intends to welcome the next empero?"

"You assume we are behind those attacks," Admiral Jiordson said in a flat voice.

"Are you not?" Corandisham's ears flicked. "We do not recognize the vessels, but we know that style of strike. Everything about their targets and strategies speak of Pyrean Navy and its Piracy Division. We will have our meeting with the Pyrean Navy, and you can answer again there, but I will allow you this opportunity to speak now as a sign of good faith. Admiral Jiordson, please explain who is behind these attacks if the Pyrean Navy is not involved."

Admiral Jiordson kept his expression neutral, but Alan knew how dangerous the situation had become. The admiral needed to answer to prevent further deterioration of relations with the Moon Empire, but Sebastian had to decide how much to tell Corandisham — a choice made harder since he still suspected the ma'jenn might be behind the attacks on pyrean vessels. Either the pyreans had failed to recognize and quell a growing piracy problem, or this whole situation was a bluff by the Moon Empire. Either way, a wrong assumption would be costly.

A small, petty part of Alan enjoyed seeing the admiral humbled after the whole debacle of the conference, but Alan didn't envy Sebastian's position, nor did he want to worsen interspecies relations. Yet intervening meant taking a gamble of his own.

"High Priest Corandisham," Alan said with a formal bow. "Forgive my interruption, but I believe I can explain the situation if you will give me the opportunity."

Corandisham's ears flickered in obvious surprise when they realized a human was standing on the bridge of a pyrean military vessel.

"Human?" They said the word with obvious distaste.

Unlike Sven or Sebastian, Alan did not rise from his bow. It was dangerous trying to engage such a highly ranked ma'jenn as a human when the HIA had no formal relationship with the Moon Empire. The ma'jenn valued propriety more than anything else, but Alan counted on curiosity getting the better of High Priest Corandisham.

Before Corandisham could reject Alan out of hand, Sven joined Alan with his own low, polite bow. "I beg you, High Priest Corandisham, I know this must seem unorthodox, but we brought Elite Inspector Alan Beringer on board the Merry Swallow for this purpose."

Alan had to force down a smile of amusement. The irony was not lost on Alan, but he agreed with Sven that sometimes a reasonable, logical narrative was more palatable than the nonsensical chaos of reality.

"Elite Inspector?" Corandisham's attitude shifted ever so slightly, as they returned to their seat. It seemed the Elite's reputation proceeded them, reaching even the Crescent Moon Court in the heart of the Empire. "Very well, Elite Inspector Beringer. Please share your findings with us."

Alan could feel Admiral Jiordson's eye boring into him, but the admiral would have to hold his peace for now. Interrupting or shutting down Alan when a high priest asked him to speak would put the pyreans into an even worse spot. And regardless of anything else, Alan worked for the Elite — not the Pyrean Navy. His mission hadn't changed since boarding the Swallow.

"High Priest Corandisham, I do not have conclusive evidence at this point, but I believe that both pyreans and humans are involved in these attacks," Alan said, cutting to the chase. "And the ma'jenn are not the only victims. The Pyrean Navy has been targeted as well."

He could feel everyone staring at him. He didn't need to turn to know that Sebastian's single green eye was boring into his back, but Alan was used to this sort of reaction. Thus he tried to imagine this was a typical assignment and not one involving a delicate political situation with both high-ranking pyreans and ma'jenn.

"What makes you believe humans are involved?" Corandisham asked.

Alan explained, "I suspect at least some human involvement as the vessels have similar energy patterns to several classes of human-made ships. My cross-checks with the available data on pyrean and ma'jenn vessels reveals nothing similar. If the operation were entirely pyrean or ma'jenn, I wouldn't see a reason to favor human technologies and manufacturing techniques."

"Maybe they want to implicate humans or confuse the investigation?" Corandisham offered as a counterpoint.

Alan admitted, "It's a possibility, and I will certainly not discount it, but that seems like a major loss in ship capabilities for relatively little gain. I prefer to investigate the more straightforward solutions until those prove inviable. The straightforward reason for these pirates to use vessels built according to human specifications is because human manufacturers are involved in their construction."

"The ships they're similar to — they are your naval vessels?" Corandisham asked.

"Not at all, High Priest," Alan replied. "The energy signal resembles an older, commercial technology rather than anything military. Such classes of vessel are common for mass manufactured long-range ships. They would normally be in the shipping sector — nothing so ominous as a warship.

"But unlike a typical shipping vessel, these ships are heavily armed, and some of the onboard technologies — the jamming systems for example — have no known corollaries to any of our existing technologies. This suggests our perpetrators have custom-built vessels, and they must have either pyrean or ma'jenn engines as they can Gate."

As Corandisham considered this information, Alan continued, "I caution you that, as of now, this is nothing but specula-tion, but I am working under the assumption that a human organization with enough capital to shoulder the costs of ship manufacturing and modification must be assisting our perpetra-tors, whom I believe are either entirely — or primarily — pyreans with some connections to the Navy."

Alan could hear Sebastian's breath catch, but Corandisham's ears tilted forward with increased interest. They leaned their cheek against the back of a hand. "An interesting theory, but one that will take deeper investigation to confirm or deny. Fortunately the Elite are well-positioned to investigate your human organizations. But what of the pyreans? I've never heard of human vessels using pyrean technology in this way. Does this mean it is not just pyrean sailors but engineers and scientists as well?"

"I believe that is the case," Alan agreed. "As you already suggested, the vessels in question employ classic naval tactics. Professor Jiordson, an expert on military strategy, has confirmed this." Alan waited for Idel to finish her bow of acknowledgment before pressing on, "I have no doubt that naval sailors are in some way involved, so it's not a stretch to imagine they have pyrean engineers and scientists are as well. Everything about this situation suggests an information leak within the Navy, which humans couldn't have breached without inside help."

"Couldn't humans have stolen that technology?" Coran-disham observed. "I am not doubting that pyreans are involved, but the Empire has dealt with many cases of human espionage seeking to steal our technology."

"It is a possibility," Alan agreed. "But the Pyrean Navy has no records of leaked documents related to Gate technologies that have reached human hands, nor have I heard of any scientific developments within any human organizations that would reflect such a technological advancement. That's why I find it more likely that dissident pyreans walked out of the Navy databases with the intel themselves before forming an alliance with human partners."

Corandisham's fingernails drummed against the captain's chair as they considered Alan's assessment. "These are interesting theories, Elite Inspector Beringer." Corandisham's ears flicked, their head tilting just enough that violet eyes shone golden for an instant. "I assume you have evidence to back them up?"

"Not much," Alan admitted. "This is a working theory. My investigation only started. Yet these mystery ships appear to have qualities of both human and pyrean vessels, and an interspecies confederacy of pirates is not unheard of — even if the involvement of rogue agents from the Pyrean Navy and one of Earth's Heavy Industries is unprecedented."

"And what of the ma'jenn?" Corandisham interjected. "You didn't mention my people as your immediate suspects. Is that because you don't believe the ma'jenn are involved in this supposed confederacy, or because you are afraid to offend me?"

Corandisham was toying with him. Alan didn't need to be an expert on the ma'jenn to know that much. Alan was being tested. To what end Alan couldn't say, but he was an inspector — not a politician. There was no need to play these games.

"At this time, there is very little evidence to suggest ma'jenn involvement. But yes, if it makes you feel better, High Priest Corandisham, I have not entirely dismissed the possibility. To conduct a successful investigation means approaching problems with an open mind."

"Good," Corandisham murmured. "Very good. Your words match your tail. That is a quality I appreciate in any sort of partnership."

Alan visibly froze, eyes widening. The shock in the room was palatable as well.

"High Priest Corandisham, I'm not sure what you —"

"It means," Corandisham cut in, "That you will report your findings to me personally in addition to your human and pyrean masters. If your theories are correct, this is a matter that concerns all three of our species, and on a personal note, I look forward to seeing your process as you build your case."

Alan could see Admiral Jiordson stiffen out the corner of his eye. Alan didn't smile, but he took a moment to savor the smug feeling of victory. Alan had kept his temper under control for the past three days, enduring slight after slight from the Navy admirals for Sven's sake, but the disrespect shown to both him and Sven was not something Alan would forget or forgive soon.

Petty enjoyment aside, Alan didn't have the faintest idea what Elite protocol would be in this scenario, but he was relatively certain the Chief Inspector would not want him to offend a member of the Crescent Moon Court regardless of the HIA's bureaucracy. And really, what was one more report to file on top of all this existing paperwork?

Alan bowed. "You honor me, High Priest Corandisham. I will endeavor to live up to your expectations."

"Please see that you do, Elite Inspector Beringer." Corandisham leaned back in their seat. Their expression looked decidedly shrewd as they asked, "But tell me, Elite Inspector Beringer, how exactly did you arrive here? I remember when humans first made contact with the pyreans. In the centuries since, I have never heard of an Elite, or any human, working with the Pyrean Navy."

"I fear that story is long and tedious," Alan said as humbly as he could manage. "But it was Captain Jiordson who proposed this arrangment. I only recently started working with the Pyrean Navy. In all honesty, I was not aware that attacks were happening on ma'jenn vessels before now. I suspect when I continue this investigation into human territories, I will discover many of the strikes that we assumed were standard Piracy Division...er, 'tolls' were undertaken by this same group of bandits."

Corandisham steepled their fingers. Even through the viewscreen, Alan could see their nails, coated in black and gold lacquer and as long and as sharp as talons. Much less cute now that Corandisham was staring at him with that piercing expression.

"So you are telling me, Elite Inspector Beringer, that the Pyrean Navy has so failed to keep this pirate confederacy under control that they were forced to recruit the help of the human Elite?"

Admiral Jiordson opened his mouth to protest, but Alan cut in before the other man could speak. "That is an overly cynical view of the situation, High Priest Corandisham, but you are...not strictly wrong."

If looks could kill, Admiral Jiordson may well have just committed homicide, but Alan was safe for now. Alan ignored the glare.

"Needless to say, High Priest Corandisham," Alan added. "I am working as an attaché to the Pyrean Navy to lend my aid in this matter. It is my duty to uncover and ultimately shut down this operation. The Elite have only one agenda — ending space piracy in all forms to allow safe, interstellar travel for all. Regardless of which species or powers are involved in this confederacy, I will do everything I can to end it."

"An honorable sentiment, Elite Inspector Beringer," Corandisham nodded. Their tone softened, and their ears turned all the way forward, the feathery tufts at the ends standing straight up. Approval, perhaps. Whatever test Alan was taking, he could only hope it was going well.

"When the ma'jenn first encountered humans, we found our interactions with your species...distasteful. We determined your race to be too violent and paranoid to engage in formal relations. It has been many generations for humans, but while I was not there personally, I remember first contact. It was not a pleasant experience for anyone."

Alan tried not to wince. Corandisham's words were an understatement. First-hand reports were hard to find from that era, but it didn't take a detective to glean that humanity had not been the heroes. Casualties had been low by human standards, but only because the ma'jenn had no concept of retaliation beyond immediate self defense. Yet those initial conflicts had locked humanity out of ma'jenn trade routes for the past three centuries. It meant that humanity remained at the whims of the pyreans and was little more than a second-class citizen in the interstellar community.

"That said," Corandisham continued, "I am not so narrow-minded as to imagine all humans conduct themselves with the dishonor that your early scouting parties did. The Elite have begun to earn a reputation of impartiality and fairness, and I am pleased to find you live up to those ideals, Elite Inspector Beringer. I look forward to seeing the progress of your investigation. If I determine that humans have grown as a species since our previous encounter, I will consider discussing more formal relations with the Empress, may Her Light ever shine on the Empire."

Alan made another gracious bow, but his heart raced faster than before. As the Elite Attaché Inspector of Observation, Alan had received a pay raise, but even this was not enough to be positioned at the heart of Moon Empire politics. Yet somehow he'd stumbled into the role of ambassador for his entire species with the fate of future interstellar relations hinging on his ability both to solve this case and not offend the ma'jenn — the latter task being one humans had historically failed at on multiple, dramatic occasions.

"You honor me, High Priest Corandisham," Alan said, "and I will do as you ask. But I am merely an inspector. Questions of diplomacy and human-ma'jenn relations would be better handled by HIA ambassadors."

"I respectfully disagree, Elite Inspector Beringer," Corandisham replied before turning to Admiral Jiordson. "Admiral Jiordson, we will speak again at the summit."

All three Jiordsons bowed as the transmission cut out.

"Connection closed, Captain." Ragnar's voice ended the oppressive silence on the bridge.

"Thank the stars that's over," Sven sighed, slumping in his usual, overly dramatic way. "A high priest out here? And coming to chastise us. I thought I was ready for a lot of things today, but this was not one of them."

"Meeting room, now," Admiral Jiordson growled. He gave

Alan a hard, wrathful look, which confirmed everything Alan had already assumed. "You too, *Inspector* Beringer."

ONCE THE DOOR to the meeting room closed, giving Alan and the three Jiordsons some amount of privacy, Sebastian's cold, collected facade dropped, and his lips curled into a savage grimace.

"Arrogant mutts," he grunted with barely contained anger. "Throwing the weight of the Court around to intimidate us? These attacks are just an excuse to renegotiate trade. And you." He turned his baleful eye toward Alan. "How dare you discuss pyrean concerns before the ma'jenn? You had no right to talk about our affairs with them."

Alan knew better than to answer, but from Sven's expression, he was about to say something everyone would regret. Yet before either Sven or Alan could speak, Idel opened her fan with a loud *crack*.

"Seb, my love, I worry you've been an admiral too long," she said in a soft, considering tone. "You're forgetting what it means to be a sailor."

"Idel, not now."

"People have died in these attacks," she continued in a low voice. "Pyrean, ma'jenn, and likely human. Why are you so concerned about some petty political maneuvering, when Inspector Beringer has accomplished more in these past few days than your Pyre-based teams have in months?"

"Ida, please —"

Idel regarded the edge of her fan before snapping it shut. "Sebastian, did you really become an admiral to play games, or are you going to try fixing the problem the Navy asked you to fix?"

From Sebastian's earlier seething fury, Alan half-expected him to return his wife's cutting words in kind, but the admiral's eye locked with hers for a long moment before he shook his head.

"However you may dislike it, Ida, these 'games' concern the

future of Pyre — the future of our people. My task was to consider the long-term ramifications of this situation. More is on the line than unsanctioned strikes."

"What, so the lives of the victims are just unfortunate side issues?" Up until now, Idel had been her usual calm, collected self, but these words held more ire than Alan had seen her express in the past three days. "That's a copout, Seb, and you know it."

"You may have left the admiralty," Sebastian countered. "But I did not."

He looked about to say something else, but after glancing in Alan's direction, he seemed to think better of it.

With a sigh, Sebastian redirected the conversation. "Regardless, this is not the time or place." He fixed his eye on Alan. "Inspector Beringer, I take back my accusations. I understand it is within your purview as an Elite investigator to discuss the case as you see fit. And your help is appreciated. We were wrong to dismiss your concerns. I apologize on behalf of myself and the rest of the admiralty."

Alan glanced at Sven, before deciding this situation would be less strange if he pretended this were a normal case and Admiral Jiordson were a normal partner.

Alan gave the admiral a respectful nod, keeping his tone formal. "I understand you have considerations beyond the investigation itself. I look forward to working with you and your team, Admiral."

Admiral Jiordson regarded Alan with a look that indicated he thought Alan was mocking him, but Alan kept his face neutral. At last Sebastian sighed — this time with open exasperation.

"I was surprised at first when I heard Tristan's descendant had join the human Elite," Sebastian admitted. "But seeing you and thinking about it more, it all makes perfect sense."

His face softened just enough that Alan felt comfortable cracking a wry smile. "What? Do you think I'm rebelling or following in his footsteps?"

"Both," Sebastian replied. "It's just like Tristan to do both at the same time."

"I suppose you're going to tell me I look like him?"

Sebastian cocked his head as if considering. "Not really, but now that you mention it, I suppose you have the same eyes." Alan must have made a face, because Sebastian immediately added, as if to reassure him, "But don't worry. He smiles more."

EPILOGUE

"Sounds like you had a busy week," Natalia said with a lazy yawn.

She was sprawled out on a grassy patch of the gardens, eyes fixed on the stars above them. Now that "evening" approached and the greenhouse lights had dimmed, the light of the galaxy was visible through the domed glass.

Natalia looked more smug than sympathetic, though, as she added, "Must be why Mama's chiding was so half-hearted."

She'd managed to avoid most of the family reunion in the exact way that Sven had not.

Sven managed a weary smile as he folded his hands behind his head. "There was a lot of chiding going around. Needed to save her strength."

He glanced over at Alan who sat beside them. Despite the fading light, the human was still inspecting Drachewunden — giving it the last bit of maintenance and polish despite the black blade already fading into the darkness — but Sven didn't comment. He felt proud that he'd managed to drag the Elite inspector away from his work even this much.

Sven had realized early into their relationship that Alan was the sort of person who liked to stay busy, but it was just as clear that this case was the most stressful, high-stakes investigation of Alan's career. Through yet another peculiar series of events, Alan was now personally and solely responsible for the promotion of human relations with both pyreans and ma'jenn — and not just any ma'jenn hive. Alan had gained access to an ear within the Crescent Court itself, which was a feat not even the pyreans had managed in their several millennia of contact with the ma'jenn.

It was so typically "Alan" to have this sort of thing happen, Sven was both impressed and amused. He could only imagine the sorts of chuckles the Fates had as they weaved Alan's skein of life. A dutiful human without ambition born to change the fate of his people. Alan wouldn't appreciate the joke, but what Sven understood and what Alan seemed to miss was that this was what made him the ideal man for the job.

Sven mused, "Alan was the only one spared Mama's chiding now that I think about it."

Alan glanced over Drachewunden one last time before giving up with a sigh and sheathing the blade. He slouched forward, cross-legged, to rest his chin on a hand. "It was certainly a pleasure to work with her, but I'm a little concerned I ruined their marriage."

"Oh, you mean their fights about the admiralty?" Natalia asked with a dismissive wave. "No, that's basically always a disagreement waiting to happen. Comes up every time Daddy asks Mama to assist him on these missions."

"Every time?" Alan's face was obscured by the darkness, but Sven could imagine his expression of incredulity.

"Every time," Sven answered with a grave nod. "Mama retired from the Navy for a reason. She felt the admiralty was too political and not focused on the common good brought through star sailing. Dad probably agrees with her to some extent, or at least respects her difference of opinion. After all, he asks her to come as his outside consultant on a lot of missions. But they inevitably argue when they're working together." Sven paused in consideration before adding, "So don't worry. It's not you, and it doesn't bother me and Nat. I don't even think it's a bad thing. It's part of why and how they love each other."

Nat gave an affirmative grunt. "May not sound that romantic, but I don't think there's anyone in the galaxy either of them respects as much as they respect each other."

"That's quite the relationship," Alan said in a soft, amused voice.

"Yeah, it sure is," Natalia said with a sigh. "But as much as I love them, and as much as I think they're incredible people, I'm also happy when they're on their way." She paused before adding in a hopeful tone, "Does this mean we're gonna be hunting pirates as our next assignment?"

"'Our' assignment, huh?" Sven gave her a mischievous grin. "You're just a hanger-on, remember?"

"Yes, well, your assignment then," Nat replied with a sniff.

"Yep, it's looking like it." Sven smiled. "Everyone's wanting to see what this Elite inspector can do — human, pyrean, and now ma'jenn. No pressure, Alan."

"None at all," Alan murmured in a droll tone.

"We have some shore leave coming up first at least," Sven said in an encouraging tone, but when Alan just rubbed the bridge of his nose, Sven couldn't help adding, "No rest in the Piracy Division, eh? Always wrongs to right somewhere in the galaxy."

Sven admired the twinkling of the stars above them. There was a lot of work to be done, but in this moment he was enjoying the soft grass beneath him, the shining stars above him, and the company of Natalia and Alan.

Alan sighed. "You know, I still have trouble accepting someone like Corandisham, a member of the Crescent Moon Court itself, can talk about 'tolls' as though the Pyrean Navy's Piracy Division is a legitimate organization and not a collection of criminals."

"Ah, you words wound me, Sir," Sven exclaimed with mock hurt. "We've been trying to explain how we are the true defenders of the galaxy to humans for centuries, but you never believe us."

"But that's what makes humans so charming, isn't it?" Natalia quipped. She sat up. Even in the starlight twinkle, her ear-to-ear smile was visible. "Did you know, Alan? According to pyrean lore, during first contact between ma'jenn and pyreans, the pyreans told the ma'jenn that this was pyrean starspace, and the ma'jenn paid the toll without asking any questions."

"That sounds apocryphal," Alana remarked.

Sven shrugged. "Maybe, but it's true that ma'jenn love rules and regulations. They're a very orderly species. Supposedly the pyreans kept trying to take ma'jenn money in more and more outlandish ways to see what the ma'jenn would do, but as long as no ma'jenn were hurt in the exchanges, the ma'jenn didn't seem to mind how the pyreans behaved."

"And thus the Navy's formalized acts of piracy were born?"

"Yes and no," Natalia corrected. "The rules were codified when humans came onto the scene. The first time we could properly communicate our intents, we asked for money the same way we did with the ma'jenn, but unlike the ma'jenn, the humans started shooting at us."

Alan pinched the bridge of his nose with a sigh. "Yes, yes, we can at least agree on those events. First contact devolved into a space battle, we were outgunned, and our ship was defeated. Our crew was spared, but everything that wasn't nailed down was taken, including the engine. Which was probably nailed down, now that I think about it."

"And then we towed your ship back to the nearest human Gate," Natalia added in a surly tone. "I don't think you ever thanked us for that act of kindness either."

"I wouldn't hold your breath on that one, Natalia," Alan replied wryly.

"But here we are, working together at last," Sven murmured. He rolled on his side to face Alan.

Sven couldn't help stealing a glance at his companion. Even in the soft starlight, the man was unreasonably handsome. Sven liked to pretend he'd kidnapped Alan for some greater, more noble purpose than just thinking he had a nice-looking face and an interesting sword, but while Sven was happy to lie to others, he wasn't one to lie to himself. He could feel Natalia's smug grin burning into his back as though she knew his every thought.

Of course Nat had figured it out. Valt and Ian had almost certainly guessed as well by now — as had Sven's mom given the way she'd hugged him, whispering into his ear "you picked a good one, Sven" before disembarking the Swallow.

Only Alan remained oblivious, which was quite a feat given he was both a detective (a pretty good one at that) and seemed to have high emotional intelligence in every other arena. Maybe it was a human thing. Either way, seeing someone be so smart and so stupid at the same time was equal parts frustrating and charming.

Alan met Sven's eyes and gave him a soft, knowing smile as if they were sharing some inside joke. Despite himself, Sven's heart leapt. It was as if he were back on his first shore leave, and he prayed to the stars it was dark enough that Alan couldn't see the heat rising through his face and flushing his ears.

"It'll be my pleasure to work with you, Captain Jiordson," Alan said, and only he could somehow say such words while being completely oblivious to how much it sounded like innu-endo. Natalia's quiet, knowing grins turned into muffled laughter, which Sven didn't appreciate one bit.

Yet Alan, Great Mother protect him, didn't seem to notice. He met Sven's gaze, brown eyes gleaming with a teasing sharpness that made Sven's heart skip again.

"But step out of line, Jiordson," Alan added, "and I won't hesitate to arrest you. I'm still an Elite inspector, after all."

Sven was trying to figure out how to reply without it sounding awkward or dirty, but he was too slow.

Nat quipped, "Be careful or he'll take you up on that, Alan."

She proceeded to dissolve into howls of laughter.

Alan looked confused, and Sven sighed, hiding his face behind his hands. Hilde would have laughed at Sven too, but she'd have been nicer about it. Yet despite Natalia's mockery, her laughter was infectious. Sven found himself smiling before allowing himself a couple weak, self-deprecating chuckles.

He peaked between his fingers to give her an affectionate look. Sven knew he was a fool, yes, but there were worse things to be, and there were worse places to be. And for all his foolishness, the Fates had granted Sven most of what he'd wanted — if not exactly as he'd expected.

Ignoring Natalia's soft cackles, Sven turned to smile back at Alan. "Then I'll endeavor to violate as little interstellar law as I can manage, Inspector."

Alan looked doubtful, and if Sven were entirely honest, Sven didn't mean it anyway.

Bonus Content

Thank you for enjoying the first book of the Triple Strike light novel series! This story was originally a comic written in high school, but it has been substantially updated to be...more like a functional novel with a coherent plot and stuff?

That said, if you were thinking "huh, this is kind of anime" you're not wrong. See if you can find all the 90s-and-earlier anime influences as a fun exploration of the writer's psyche! (Hint: yes, I have adored Leiji Matsumoto since childhood).

Regardless, please enjoy some bonus content created just for the novelization!

Until next time!

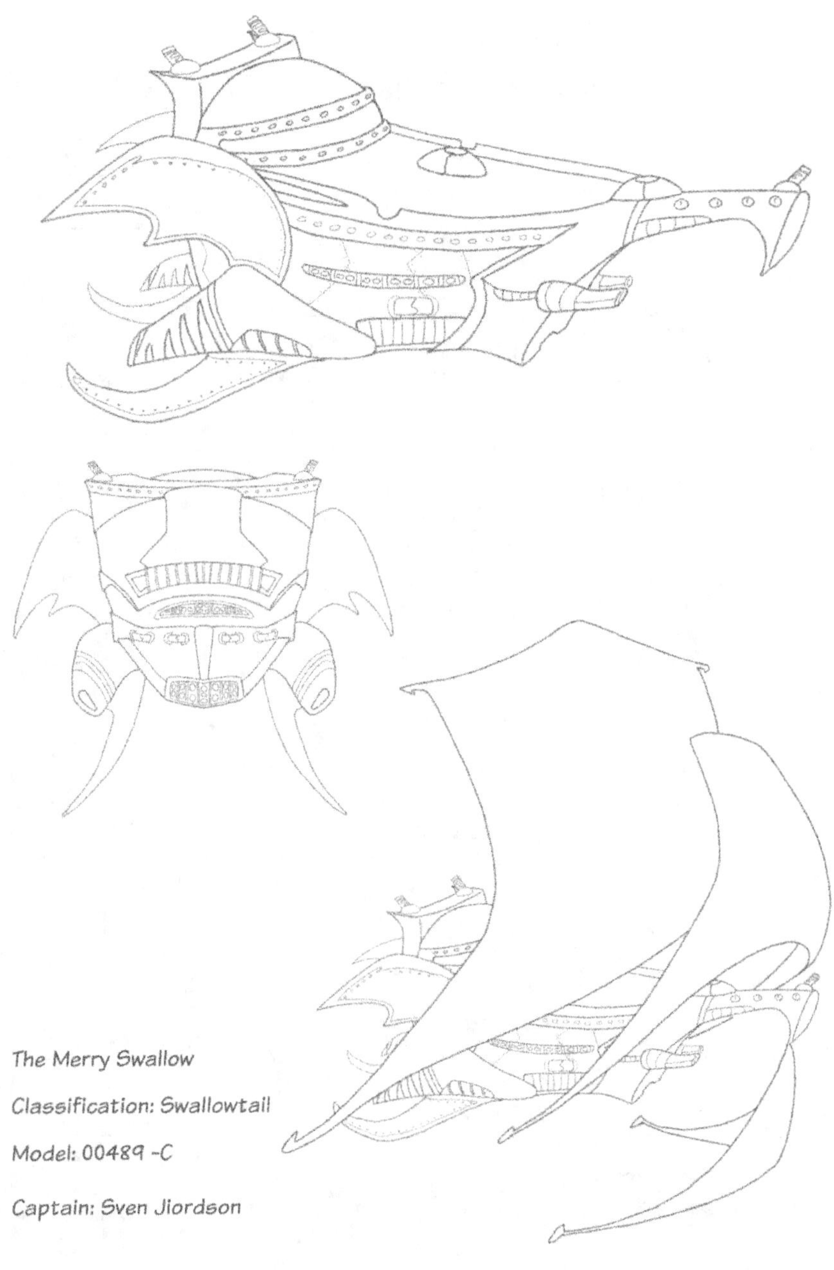

The Merry Swallow

Classification: Swallowtail

Model: 00489 -C

Captain: Sven Jiordson

Officers of the Merry Swallow

Engineers of the Merry Swallow

Sif Roen

Kennan al'Qin

Agnus nie Tiernan

Dirk Ferren

Lance Ferren

Chapter 3 Bonus:
A Difference In Perspective

Alan's Thoughts:

So now Sven's seen my Black Dragon tattoo. He must think I'm a hypocrite... this whole time I've denied my pyrean heritage but here I am carrying the Volsung family sword and wearing the Volsung family tattoo like some sort of proud pyrean star sailor. I can't bear th

Sven's Thoughts:

How is he so hot?

Jiordsons ranked by "how bad of an idea is it to wager against them"
5 Sebastian: A safe bet
Honorable and straight forward.
Is dead.
4 Hildegarde: A safe bet
3 Sven: Risky
May be calculating. May be an idiot.
Loves deception and loop-holes.
2 Natalia: Risky
1 Idel: Don't
Treats even friendly competition as a life-or-death battle. Will actually destroy you.

Thank you for reading!

G.M. Gray was born to a small, middle class family of wolves. Although originally given an unpronounceable wolf name, Gray took on the agnomen "Gun Metal" after the death of their beloved Metal Gear Solid 4 Limited Collector's Edition Playstation 3. While the previous sentences are mostly fake facts (G.M.'s MGS4 Limited Collector's Edition PS3 did actually die), Gray does live a real life made of real, true facts. True facts include: teaches computer science at a university, has an apiary and too many (just enough) guinea pigs, used to fence, and loves both 19th Century and Silver Age Russian literature...as well as anime (naturally). For G.M. Gray, light novels seem as good a way as any to explore all of the above interests.

Coming Soon! Triple Strike: Pasts Revisited

Alan Beringer's adventures on the Merry Swallow continue as he investigates the mysterious pirate confederacy on behalf of not one but all three starfaring species. Despite his human heritage and this high-stakes assignment, Alan's friendships with the crew deepen — not the least of which being his relationship with the captain, Sven Jiordson, whose infatuation with Alan is obvious to everyone...except Alan.

Yet this situation becomes more tenuous as the Fates entangle them with threads of their pasts. As Alan faces his fiancée from an arranged marriage they are both avoiding, and Sven tries to come to terms with his feelings, the powers within the confederacy start to move against Alan and the crew. Not only must Alan navigate a trap that could leave him marked a traitor against humanity, events from thirty years earlier may prove just as deadly now as they were then.

While Alan is far too sensible to want to fall in love in the midst of all this chaos, he may not have much of a choice — assuming he lives long enough to realize it!

Alan took a step toward the other man, but Sven brushed past him to look out the porthole. Sven folded his arms behind his back as he considered the stars that surrounded the ship.

"You're very pyrean, you know that, Alan?"

"Um…what?" Alan blinked.

Until now, Alan had assumed he knew where this conversation was going. He'd assumed Sven was still upset from what had happened on 3rd Daphne. Alan had hurt Sven's feelings — that much was obvious. He'd assumed Sven was frustrated. He'd assumed they'd talk about it, Alan would apologize, and then they'd move on.

But now that none of this was happening, Alan didn't know what to expect. He couldn't guess what Sven was thinking.

Sensing Alan's confusion, Sven clarified, "At least, you have many qualities that pyreans idealize."

Alan shook his head. "Er, which qualities do you mean? Fun-loving? Cheerful? Fatalistic? Alcoholic? I'm sorry, Sven, but I'm not really any of those. I'm pretty sure I'm nothing more than a stodgy human nobleman."

"You're brave," Sven insisted, turning to face Alan. "You live without regrets."

Alan laughed, but Sven's bright eyes regarded him with a hooded look as if that hadn't been a joke. Alan's smile faded.

"Sven, what's gotten into you? That's not true at all. You know me better than that. "

"I'm not sure I do, Alan," Sven admitted. "But I would like to."

Something about the way Sven's voice softened made Alan shiver. Sven's green eyes gleamed in the low lights of the cabin, piercing Alan with a dark and pressing intimacy.

"Your eyes are in the present," Sven murmured, voice barely above a whisper.

Eyes in the present. It was an old pyrean idiom, roughly translating to 'living in the moment,' but it went deeper than that. Someone with eyes in the present was a person who'd accepted the entire skein of their life. Such a person knew that both past and future had been determined long ago, and thus they anticipated nothing. To have eyes in the present meant someone experienced the fullness of life, the freshness of breathing, and the essence of existence. It was the highest compliment a pyrean could pay another.

"Sven —"

"I keep trying to see in the present," Sven continued, cutting Alan off. "But my eyes are either in the past or the future. When I think about this mission, I see Hilde. I see all the things I lost and all the things I'm afraid to lose again. And when I try not to think about this mission, I think about you...the Elite Inspector on board my ship."

Sven trailed off, turning to gaze out the porthole. His words held such quiet intensity, Alan felt his heart thump in his chest.

"When all this is over," Sven said, voice still soft. "When you're no longer assigned to the Swallow as part of your Elite duties, what will you do, Alan?"

"I..." Alan started, but he trailed off as if he didn't know the answer. Yet it was obvious what he'd do. There was only one answer — so logical and straightforward there was no need to hesitate.

"I'll follow my orders, and go wherever they ask me to, I suppose." Simple and uncomplicated. Why then did the words taste like ash on his tongue?

Sven turned to face Alan. A bright smile touched Sven's lips, but his eyes held pain — grief. It was plain to see, despite the way Sven smoothed his features as soon as Alan noticed.

"This is what I mean," Sven said in a teasing tone. "This is why you're so pyrean."